KT-482-121

800207735

HER BILLIONAIRE
PROTECTOR

HER BILLIONAIRE PROTECTOR

NINA SINGH

MILLS & BOON

All rights reserved including the right of reproduction in whole or in part in any form. This edition is published by arrangement with Harlequin Books S.A.

This is a work of fiction. Names, characters, places, locations and incidents are purely fictional and bear no relationship to any real life individuals, living or dead, or to any actual places, business establishments, locations, events or incidents. Any resemblance is entirely coincidental.

This book is sold subject to the condition that it shall not, by way of trade or otherwise, be lent, resold, hired out or otherwise circulated without the prior consent of the publisher in any form of binding or cover other than that in which it is published and without a similar condition including this condition being imposed on the subsequent purchaser.

® and TM are trademarks owned and used by the trademark owner and/or its licensee. Trademarks marked with ® are registered with the United Kingdom Patent Office and/or the Office for Harmonisation in the Internal Market and in other countries.

First published in Great Britain 2020
by Mills & Boon, an imprint of HarperCollins*Publishers*
1 London Bridge Street, London, SE1 9GF

Large Print edition 2020

© 2020 Nilay Nina Singh

ISBN: 978-0-263-08487-0

MIX
Paper from
responsible sources
FSC C007454

This book is produced from independently certified FSC™ paper to ensure responsible forest management. For more information visit www.harpercollins.co.uk/green.

Printed and bound in Great Britain
by CPI Group (UK) Ltd, Croydon, CR0 4YY

For Becks,
for all the joy you've brought us.
And the way you guard us
in your own way.

CHAPTER ONE

ADAM STEELE KNEW he was in the right line of work. But days like this, he wondered if perhaps he should have gone in a different professional direction. He had no right to complain. Providing personal security for the A-listers of the world as CEO of Steele Security Services had certainly provided him with all sorts of riches, both material and personal. But every once in a while, an assignment arose that he just knew was going to be a giant pain in the—

Before he could complete the thought, the elevator pinged and the shiny stainless steel doors swished open. Adam entered the empty elevator and punched in the number to the top floor.

Assignments borne of requests for personal favors always made him wary. That personal connection often led to complications and distractions. And distractions could be deadly in his line of work.

He should have turned Brant down as soon as

his friend had asked to see him. Instead, here he was at Terrance Technology headquarters about to meet with his old friend and the senior Mr. Terrance to personally discuss why they were suddenly interested in his services. Something told him it would be a meeting he would ultimately regret.

But Brant didn't often take no for an answer. Adam had learned that during the years they'd served together and even before that. They'd been friends since middle school. And he remembered his friend's character well, even though those days seemed like another lifetime.

Adam tried to avert the images threatening to invade his mind by focusing on the view of the greater Dallas metropolitan area outside the glass elevator as it took him up. Images of war-torn buildings and hot desert…

Brant made his home mostly in Manhattan these days. The fact that he'd made this trip simply to see Adam face-to-face said a lot about the importance of whatever it was he wanted to discuss.

The elevator finally came to a stop and the doors opened with a smooth swoosh. A statuesque blonde woman immediately stood up from behind a long, cherrywood desk across from him. Her tall heels clicked loudly on the heavily varnished floor as she approached him. She looked like she could be gracing the runway at a high-end fashion show. Adam would know; he'd been in charge of security for several such shows in the past.

"You must be Mr. Steele," she said through a brilliant, ivory-white smile. "I'll walk you to Mr. Terrance's office. They're waiting for you."

Adam gave her a slight nod before following her past her desk and down a wide corridor.

"Can I get you anything? Coffee? Or water?" the woman asked over her shoulder. "Something else?"

Adam didn't miss the flirtatious flip of her hair as she added that last part, nor the implication in her tone. Any other time, he might have pursued her invitation. Right now, he had too much on his mind.

"No. Thank you."

Her small shrug was barely noticeable as they reached a tall wooden door that stood slightly ajar. With a small knock, she pushed the door open and motioned for him to step inside.

Two impeccably groomed men in well-tailored suits immediately stood up from behind an elegant desk as soon as he entered. They had the same eyes in shape and color. Anyone who gave them a thorough glance would easily conclude that they were father and son.

Brant stepped up to him with a wide grin and he suddenly found himself in a tight embrace. "Adam, man. It's been way too long." Brant stepped back to study him. "You're still as ugly as I remember."

Adam laughed. It was a wonder the two of them had become such close friends over the years despite the odds. Brant was a prodigal son, born into wealth and a loving family. Adam had been abandoned and discarded when he was barely a teen. If not for the decency of a well-off uncle who'd begrudgingly taken him in, Adam would have no doubt found himself in the foster system instead of the ritzy town where he'd grown up. A town where he'd known he didn't fit in.

"Nah. You're just too pretty for your own good." Adam rebutted. The teasing words held a minutia of truth. Brant had the reddish-blond, blue-eyed looks of a Renaissance angel.

Though somehow, he carried such features without looking the least bit angelic. In fact, he bore the sort of rugged looks that most men worked hard to achieve with hours in the gym and intense grooming.

"So I've been told," Brant responded. He motioned to the older man behind him. "You remember my father."

Adam reached over the desk with his hand out. "Mr. Terrance. So nice to see you again."

"Please, call me Edward. We are all adults now, after all," he said as they shook hands.

"Very well," Adam agreed, though it would take some getting used to.

All three sat down with Adam facing the other two men across the desk.

Brant took a deep breath, making it clear any catching up or chitchat would have to wait. "I'll begin by saying this might be a lot to ask, especially given that as CEO you don't personally do fieldwork anymore. And considering that you know the person in question."

That last sentence sent warning bells ringing in Adam's head.

Brant continued, "But I find the need to ask it, anyway."

Adam crossed one ankle over his knee. "Maybe you should just tell me what this is all about."

Brant inhaled sharply and looked away toward the wide window. He appeared visibly shaken. "It's Ani."

Adam tried not to react visibly to the name. It wasn't easy, despite his professional training. "Your younger sister."

"That's right."

"Has something happened? Last I heard, she was on her way to being the next international musical phenomenon." Anikita Terrance was a musical prodigy, a world-class pianist at the young age of twenty-six.

Brant nodded, pride clear in his eyes. "That she is. In fact, she's been asked to perform in Paris. Then Brussels. A one-woman concert."

"She got her talent from her mother," Edward added, the sadness thick in his voice and clear in his expression. They'd lost Brant and Ani's mother over a decade ago after an unexpected and short illness.

"Is she in trouble in some way?" Adam asked.

Brant snapped the pen he'd been holding in two. Adam didn't think he was even aware of doing so. The action spoke of far more than concern for a sibling. Brant was downright angry. Brotherly protectiveness could be a hell of a force, and Brant had always been fiercely protective of his sister, particularly after their mother had passed.

"I'm afraid she is," he finally answered, his voice shaky. "Through no fault of her own. And I trust you to be the one to get her out of it."

Ani bit down on the groan of frustration churning at the base of her throat as she entered the high-rise building in central Dallas that housed the family business headquarters. As much as she loved her brother and father—they were the only family she had, after all—this meeting was sure to be an exercise in patience.

She knew what they wanted to talk to her about. And she knew they only had her best interests in mind. Still, she couldn't help but feel they were simply blowing the matter out of all proportion. As usual. Famous people received disturbing messages all the time. Or near famous, in her case. She was hardly a household name. She was only just starting to receive some recognition for her playing.

All the more reason for Brant and her father to get a grip already. Yes, she'd received some anonymous notes and emails from someone claiming to be her only true love, her soul mate. They hadn't been overtly threatening. But Brant and her father had had a bit of a panic when the last note mentioned that her secret admirer would show himself when he felt the time was right. And that afterward, they would live happily-ever-after when he whisked her away. It was enough of a threat that the two significant males in her life were now up in arms about her "stalker."

Hence the reason she'd been summoned to her father's office to discuss it all this morning.

Ani liked to think she wasn't naive. Of course, she'd heard horror stories about seemingly innocent correspondence from admirers turning suddenly dangerous and nefarious. She just didn't think her case warranted such alarm. Not yet, anyway.

The elevator finally reached the top floor and Ani exited with a resigned sigh. Best to get this over with. The sooner she could smooth over Brant and her dad's ruffled feathers, the sooner she could focus on practicing and rehearsal for her upcoming performances in Europe. It had been a pure stroke of luck that a previous act had canceled a couple of dates on their tour. Ani's manager had been at the right place at the right time.

Her father's secretary gave her an easy smile as she waved and walked past the circular desk in the main lobby. She appeared to be handling several phone conversations at once. Her father hired no one but the best. Ani returned the smile and entered her father's office.

To her surprise, Brant and her dad weren't alone. Another man rose immediately from his chair across Dad's desk and approached her. Tall and dark, the man could be straight out of the pages of *Polo Magazine*. Dear heavens, he was certainly fit. His expertly tailored suit failed to hide the muscular frame underneath. She couldn't quite place it, but she knew him from somewhere. He had a strange sense of familiarity about him.

He held a small notebook in his hand. Understanding dawned. One of Dad's employees was apparently a fan of hers. He certainly didn't look like the typical enthusiast who attended

piano performances, but what did she know?
She was so new to all of this.

With a polite smile, Ani reached over and
took the notebook from his hand. A strange
sensation traveled through her core as her fingers brushed his. It was the barest of contact,
lasting less than a second. Yet she felt a physical tug that could only be described as longing. A curl of heat formed around the vicinity
of her belly, then moved lower. How utterly
silly. Had it been that long since she'd enjoyed
the company of the opposite sex?

She forced herself to push away the unsettling thoughts and scribbled her signature on
the page, then added a musical note symbol.
She handed him back the notebook.

He simply stood silently. Then he blinked at
her. Not even a thank-you. Was he that star-
struck? And why had the room suddenly gone
completely quiet?

Ani glanced at her father in confusion. He
was rubbing his forehead. Brant, for his part,
looked somewhat amused. Clearly, she had
missed something.

Well, if no one else was going to break the

silence… Ani summoned another smile. "It's always nice to meet a fan."

Brant let out some sort of sound behind her. Not quite a laugh, but pretty close.

Her father cleared his throat. "Ani, he's not quite a fan."

The stranger lifted an eyebrow, his gaze solidly fixed on her face. "On the contrary," he began. "I enjoy Ms. Terrance's music immensely."

There was no mistaking the slight hint of teasing in his tone. Ani wanted to sink into the floor and disappear. Whoever he was, he was most definitely not here for her autograph. She'd clearly gone ahead and flattered herself. No wonder Brant looked as if he wanted to break into laugher.

The stranger stepped closer to her and Ani had to stifle an urge to move away. The man had much too strong an enigmatic pull. And she had no doubt that he was now laughing at her inside.

"But perhaps I should introduce myself," he announced. Ani's confusion and embarrassment grew as he continued, "Or reintroduce myself, as you clearly don't seem to remember who I am."

But his name echoed in her head before he could utter it. *Of course.* Suddenly, the missing puzzle piece fell into place. Adam Steele.

How could she have not known immediately? Brant and Adam had been buddies since middle school who'd then served overseas together. He'd been a guest in their home and Ani had always felt like an awkward and clumsy teen around him. In turn, he'd seemed utterly unimpressed and annoyed by her mere presence. Probably because she stared at him like the besotted schoolgirl she'd been at the time. Apparently, her body had recognized him before her mind had, judging by her intense physical reaction.

She distinctly remembered one afternoon when she'd headed down to the family swimming pool unaware that Brant had Adam and a few other friends over for an afternoon swim. She'd barely made it onto the patio in her newly purchased two-piece swimsuit when Adam had suddenly leaped out of the pool. Not even bothering to dry off, he'd uttered some kind of excuse about why he had to leave right then.

Now, heat warmed her cheeks as she vividly remembered being unable to look away when he'd stormed past her, his chiseled chest and tanned, broad shoulders dripping wet. He hadn't even spared a glance in her direction as he'd stormed off.

Ani felt the embarrassing sting of the moment as if it had happened yesterday. Looking at him now, it was little wonder she hadn't recognized him right away. Any hint of boyishness or youthful features had vanished from his face. His ebony hair was now cut shorter than she'd ever seen on him. A dusting of dark stubble ran along his angular jawline. His eyes were harder.

Ani tried to shake off the memories. How stunningly, cringingly cliché. She'd embarrassingly had the hots for her older brother's friend. He'd been so out of her league. Unlike most of Brant's neighborhood friends, Adam had always seemed distant and unapproachable with an aura she'd be hard-pressed to describe, much rougher around the edges than the others. The perfect swoon bait for an awkward teenage girl who had no real female influence around her.

No wonder he had been her very first crush.

Clearly, she hadn't outgrown it. And she'd just made a complete fool of herself upon seeing him again.

He had to wonder if she was playing some kind of game. She couldn't really be that much of an ingenue. That description certainly might have fit Anikita Terrance all those years ago. But she'd done some growing up in the meantime. It chafed his ego a bit that she hadn't guessed who he was. And didn't that make him all sorts of foolish?

She'd thought he was here for her autograph!

In all fairness, he'd had an advantage over her, knowing who she was and why they were all here in her father's office. He had to admit, he might have very well been unable to recognize her if their roles had been reversed.

Anikita was no longer the bespectacled, gangly, awkward teenager she'd been when he'd last laid eyes on her. Just how often had he good-naturedly teased her about those thick glasses and tight ponytail?

He had nothing to tease her about now. The thick glasses were gone. Her thick, satiny red hair hung in soft waves around her face and over her shoulders. Gone were the frizzy, tight curls. And the shade was so much richer. She had inherited the most striking looks from both sides of her heritage. Dark, almond-shaped eyes from her Singaporean mother and fiery red hair from her American father. It made for a stunningly striking combination. Adam cursed internally. He was so not the type to wax poetic about the color of a woman's hair. Not normally, anyway.

He'd felt inexplicably drawn to her all those years ago. Probably because she had never questioned his background or asked where he came from. And also probably because she was one of the handful of people in this town who didn't manage to make him feel completely out of place in their well-heeled circle of friends. She and Brant had been the only ones who hadn't, in fact.

He'd also managed to see beneath Brant's little sister's geeky exterior to the attractive young woman hovering underneath. And man, had he been right. Anikita Terrance was a stunner all grown-up.

A stunner who was currently staring at him with confusion. *Focus.*

Brant suddenly approached to stand between the two of them. He looked nervous. "Adam, sorry. We haven't really had a chance to discuss all this with Ani just yet. Her schedule has just been so busy." He glanced down at his much shorter sister. "Also, she's been a little resistant to the idea."

"What idea?" Ani asked.

Adam pinched the bridge of his nose. Great. Just great. She really had no idea why he was here. Hadn't been expecting him at all. What had Brant and his father been thinking?

His friend must have sensed the frustration humming through him. "You have to understand, Adam. We weren't even sure you were on board. Then by the time Ani found some time to come in, Dad and I never got a chance to actually tell her."

"Tell me what?" Ani demanded once more.

Brant inhaled deeply before addressing his sister. "Adam owns a private security firm now."

Adam watched her facial features harden as she put two and two together. "Do you mean to tell me you're trying to keep me secure with a bodyguard?" Saying she was resistant to the idea certainly seemed to be the case, judging by the murderous look she threw at her brother. She turned just long enough to shoot the same glare at her father, who merely shrugged.

"Adam's the best there is," Brant insisted. "I'd trust him with my life, sis. And yours."

"You didn't even discuss it with me, Brant. You had no right to make such a decision." Ani didn't give her brother a chance to respond before turning back to face Adam. "I'm sorry you had to waste a trip out here, Mr. Steele. My brother and father seem to have exaggerated my predicament. I have no need for personal security."

So formal… She wasn't using his first name. For some reason, that rubbed him the wrong way. It had been bad enough when she hadn't even remembered who he was.

"You've been receiving anonymous messages from a stranger," Brant argued.

She glared at her sibling. "They've hardly been threatening."

"Not yet, anyway." Adam felt compelled to jump in.

"He's got a point, Ani. Just listen—"

Adam cut Brant off before he could continue.

"I'll leave if you like, Ms. Terrance." Two could play the formal game. "But would you mind if I asked you a couple of questions first?"

She released a deep sigh and leaned back against her father's wide mahogany desk. "I suppose. It's the least we can do given how we've wasted your time today."

Her tone gave every indication that she was merely indulging him. How generous of her. It shouldn't have irked him, but it did. He was used to dealing with some of the wealthiest, most privileged individuals on the planet. He'd seen more than his share of spoiled, entitled behavior. But coming from her, it sent prickles of irritation along his skin. He'd thought he knew her better.

"Do you have any idea who the sender might be?" he asked her.

She shook her head. "I get correspondence all the time."

"Has anyone else been as regular with their contacts as this admirer?"

She paused before answering. "No. He is the only one who emails regularly."

"How often would you say he does?"

"At least three times a week. He uses different addresses. But the sign-off is always the same. He calls himself Ani's Admirer."

"I see. When this all started, did you receive these messages with the same frequency?" When he'd first walked in, Adam had been convinced he wanted nothing to do with this assignment. That he was only here to indulge the request of a friend. So why was he now actually trying to convince Ani to hear him out?

He knew the answer, though he loathed to admit it. The moment he'd seen her, his protective instincts had kicked into high gear. The thought that she might actually be in some kind of danger wasn't sitting well, though he'd sworn to himself he wouldn't return to fieldwork. He didn't miss it at all. And the people who worked for him were more than capable without him.

But Ani was acting as if she were doing him the favor. He was downright foolish to continue standing here rather than accept the out she was giving him and simply walk away.

"No. At first he only sent them once a week or so," Ani answered.

"So things have escalated."

She crossed her arms in front of her chest. "I would hardly call a few emails an escalation."

"Have you at least changed your email address?" He couldn't seem to help the accusatory mocking in his tone.

This time, her irritation was obvious in the tight gritting of her teeth. "Of course I have. He seems to have somehow discovered what it was changed to."

"So he's determined and skilled."

The other two men in the room gasped with alarm. But Ani wasn't moved.

"Have you answered any of these emails?" Adam continued.

"Of course not."

"And what happens if he grows impatient?"

"Impatient?"

He nodded. "If he gets frustrated at your lack of response?"

"I guess we'll have to cross that bridge if we come to it." Adam didn't miss the emphasis on the *if.*

"Unless it's too late."

She defiantly lifted her chin. "Regardless, I do not need a personal bodyguard at the present." But her statement this time sounded a bit less certain, her voice wavering ever so slightly. "I simply don't see a need at this point."

He really didn't need this. So why wasn't he walking away already?

Ani stood glaring at him. Adam half expected her to stomp her foot before he gave her a small, affirmative nod. "If you say so, Ms. Terrance."

Ani had to resist the urge to stomp her foot. She most certainly didn't need a bodyguard. And she definitely didn't need him to be the overbearing, overly smug man that was Adam Steele. What nerve, to ask her if she'd taken the most basic precautions. What exactly did he take her for?

Brant and her father had really gone too far this time.

"Ani, please hear us out," her father pleaded. She hated that strain in his voice, hated that he was so worried about her. He overworried. He always had. Ever since the loss of her mother.

Adam turned to the other men. "Could we have a moment? Anikita and me. Alone?"

Ani started to protest but couldn't seem to summon any words. No way she wanted to be alone with him; her insides were quaking just being this close to him in the same room.

She was likely to blither like an idiot if he got her alone. How could she not have gotten over a silly schoolgirl crush after all these years? Adam Steele may have changed in appearance, but he was still treating her like a pesky, ignorant child.

But her father and Brant didn't even hesitate. They swiftly walked out the door, shutting it quietly behind them.

"Your father and brother are very worried about you," Adam began as soon as they were alone.

She'd thought often over the years what it might be like to run into him. The scenario currently before her had never once crossed her mind.

"They tend to worry excessively."

"Maybe so. But I know your brother well enough to sense that it's different this time. He's very concerned."

"That's because he's used to having me near home. Where he or my father can keep an eye on me. I didn't even go away for university, I stayed in Dallas. They're both out of sorts because I'll be traveling to perform. That's all there is to it."

He shrugged. "You might be right. But I'm not the type who can live with myself if Brant's concern turns out to be warranted and I just walked away."

"Even if I'm the one asking you to?"

"I'm afraid so. And then there's your father."

Sweet honey on a cracker. Why did he have to go there? "So Brant told you?"

"Only that Edward had a health scare a couple months ago."

"His heart. He's being monitored very closely. By the finest cardiothoracic specialists in Dallas."

"Still, the last thing he needs is the added worry and stress about the safety of his only daughter."

Ani felt her resolve deflate like a pinned balloon. Of course she'd thought of all that. Had almost entertained the idea of canceling her mini performance tour. But ultimately, she'd decided against canceling. If she knew her father, the thought that he'd held her back from her dream would be no less traumatizing for him than his actual concern about her traveling.

She stood and rubbed a hand down her face. "Does it...? I mean, can we...?"

He merely quirked an eyebrow at her.

Better to just say it outright. "What I'm saying is, does it have to be you?" There. She'd just gone ahead and blurted it out.

A muscle twitched along his jaw. She'd hit a nerve. No doubt he was insulted by her question. Ani had a sudden urge to cry. What must Adam think of her? He probably took her as a spoiled, rich dilettante used to getting her own way, with how she was behaving. She'd actually signed an autograph for him thinking he was a fan, for heaven's sake. Adam no doubt thought her a snob with a superiority complex.

It was so far from reality.

The truth was, her sanity would be sorely tested if Adam Steele was the one guarding her. The two of them together as she traveled for her two performance dates. In close quarters. How in the world would she even be able to concentrate on her playing? He had no idea the affect he would have on her. The havoc he might wreak on her equilibrium. As much as she wanted to deny it, and as much as she wished it weren't so, he still had an effect on her. Just as he had when they were kids.

She'd only laid eyes on him again about thirty

minutes ago and already she was behaving un-characteristically—less like the accomplished musician she was and more like the silly school-girl who'd been shooed away at every turn.

Adam's answer was abrupt, and hardness rang in his voice. "You'll have a full detail. A team of professionals. But I'm the one in charge." Clearly, there'd be no arguing that. "As competent and highly trained as they are, all of those professionals work for me."

"I see."

"I'm the best there is." There was no brag-ging or conceit in his voice. Simply a matter of truth he had no qualms stating. "Trust me, I'm the man you want at the helm."

That was it. She had no response. But she wasn't about to fold completely either. "In that case, I'll agree to a trial run."

"What's that supposed to mean?"

"You have to realize this was all thrown at me unexpectedly. I have to wrap my head around it somehow."

"What do you suggest?"

"You accompany me to the first venue. The Le Trianon theater in Paris. After that trip, I need to have a heart-to-heart with my brother and father. Perhaps bring the Dallas authorities in, see what they have to say."

He studied her. "I know what they're going to say. Would you like me to tell you?"

She simply shrugged.

"They're going to say they'll put their cyber-security guys on it. But your case will be low priority. As you said yourself, so far you're only dealing with a couple complimentary emails. After that, they'll tell you that without any specific threats or any kind of leads to go on, there isn't much they can do for you."

Ani had to fight the urge to bristle at his smug tone. "Nevertheless, it's all I can agree to at this point. You and your team accompany me to the first performance. After that, the four of us will revisit this whole matter."

He gave her an exaggerated nod that bordered on a slight bow. He was mocking her. "As you wish, Ms. Terrance."

She managed to stammer out a resigned thank-you, despite her annoyance. The man bothered her on so many levels.

I'm the man you want...

Little did he know, that was what scared her the most.

* * *

"Is this really necessary?" Ani asked in a defiant tone as she begrudgingly let Adam into her apartment.

"I'm just going to take a look around. Get a feel for your surroundings." He stepped past her through the doorway. "I'll study the outdoors on my way out when I leave."

He'd been satisfied enough by the footman at the high-rise building's entrance and the solid lock on her apartment door.

Her place wasn't quite what he would have expected. A grand piano sat in the corner. Music books were strewn about all over the floor. A book sat open on its face on the cream-colored couch that was the centerpiece of the room. Behind the piano was an open doorway that led to a small kitchen. There was a pet bed next to a water dish, and a feed bowl against the wall on the opposite side.

"You have a dog?"

She nodded. "He's at doggy day care for a few more hours."

"Good. It's good to have a pet around, under the circumstances."

She released a small laugh and her eyes lit

up with amusement. For an insane moment, Adam wished things could have been different between them. That he was somehow here to pick her up for a date and they were merely getting acquainted, learning about each other.

Maybe in a different universe.

He squashed the useless pining. Meaningful relationships with women weren't in his cards.

"He's hardly a guard dog," Ani said. "He's about twelve pounds."

Adam returned her smile. "Still, any dog is useful for alerting their owner to unexpected visitors."

She laughed again. "Right. You might change your mind about that when you see Snowball. He's more likely to lick any visitors with boundless affection."

A twelve-pound dog named Snowball. Clearly, they weren't speaking about a German shepherd or a Doberman.

He made his way to the window. Her blinds were open. Anyone in the building across the street would have an easy view into her apartment with the right eye gear. He would have to address that further with her at some point. Once they got past this trip to Paris.

He pulled his notebook out from his back pocket. "Does anyone else have a key to the apartment?"

"Just the building manager."

"No one else? A friend? The person who waters your plants?"

She shook her head. "No."

"A boyfriend?" Why was he holding his breath after asking that?

"No. I'm not seeing anyone seriously. Certainly not serious enough to share my key."

The unknotting at the base of his gut was not due to some sort of relief at her answer.

"Are you seeing anyone at all? On any dating sites? I'll need names if so."

She visibly bristled. "Is that really necessary? We seem to be getting into some personal areas here."

"It's my job to get this personal, Ani."

"Not yet, it isn't. Your assignment hasn't even begun."

"I beg to differ," he countered.

She planted her hands on her hips. "And I beg to argue."

Adam blew out a deep sigh. He wasn't going to debate the point with her. The time would come soon enough when she could no longer deny his involvement. And whether she liked it or not, he'd considered himself on the clock as soon as she'd walked into her father's office earlier.

"Nevertheless, we need to go over some ground rules."

Ani crossed her arms over her chest. "What sort of ground rules?"

"You need to keep your phone on at all times, so that I can track it."

She glared at him.

He continued, "Please forward me your password so that I can monitor your emails."

Her jaw fell open. "Some of those messages are personal."

"I'm sorry if this is uncomfortable for you. But some things are nonnegotiable."

She visibly gritted her teeth.

"Furthermore, don't make any sudden changes in plans. I need to know where you are and what you're doing at all times."

"You can't be serious. The tour hasn't even started yet."

He ignored that. "Do you have any plans for

the rest of the day? When do you leave to pick up your dog?"

"He's getting dropped off here later by the day-care staff," she answered. Adam could have sworn she hesitated before she answered. "Why?" She wanted to know.

"I told you. You're not to go anywhere without letting me know exactly where you're going and the timing."

A tinge of red appeared on her cheeks. "This is preposterous. Please tell me my father and brother didn't agree to any of this."

"It just so happens they did."

Before she could argue further, he made his way down the hall to her bedroom.

"Hey, wait a minute," she protested behind him.

He halted in his tracks at the urgency in her voice. "Is there a problem?"

She brushed past him, rubbing against his shoulder in the process. A delicate flowery scent tickled his nostrils as she moved by. "I wasn't exactly expecting company. Give me a chance to pick up some things."

Adam leaned back against the wall. He felt off balance, out of sorts. This wasn't how his usual gigs worked. Never before had he been assigned a VIP who didn't want his protection. Not to mention, he'd been out of the field for the better part of two years. It was all throwing him off. Not at all how he liked to run his game. Even the smallest mistake could be too costly.

He should have asked her for permission before trying to enter her bedroom. She probably had all sorts of personal items lying about. After all, it was probably where she undressed.

He made certain to stop that train of thought completely in its tracks.

He entered the room when she gave him the okay moments later. The shades were pulled wide open here as well.

"Do you keep these blinds open mostly?"

Her mouth formed a tight thin line. "Only when I want natural sunlight. That's their purpose after all, isn't it?"

"At all times? What if you're not dressed?"

Ani gasped.

"Did it ever occur to you that someone might be watching?"

"If you're asking if I prance around the apartment naked with my shades wide open, the answer is no. Obviously."

Adam bit out a curse. Again, he found himself redirecting the path of his thoughts. How utterly, shamefully unprofessional. What the hell was wrong with him? He'd convinced himself that he could handle this assignment because he owed it to his friend.

One thing was certain, he had to refocus and pull it together or he was bound to make a mistake. His new VIP was distracting him like none other before.

He knew firsthand and all too well exactly how costly distractions could be.

Ani watched Adam leave her apartment twenty minutes later and blew out a breath as she shut the door behind him. That had gone even worse than she'd anticipated.

He sure seemed to take up a lot of space. His mere presence in her living quarters had made her edgy and tense. She was too aware of all the pure masculinity he exuded. And when he strode into her bedroom, she'd wanted to kick herself for the wayward thoughts that had shot through her head like a mini movie. If someone had told her years ago that Adam Steele would be standing in the middle of her bedroom, she would have offered to sell them a bridge.

More was the pity, considering the frustrating reason for his presence.

She had to stop thinking of him like that. He was only a temporary fixture in her life for the next few weeks. For all the wrong reasons. Once her two-city performance tour ended, Adam would go back to being the unreachable, distant teenage crush from her past just as he'd been all along. Nothing more.

Well, he may think his responsibility toward her had already started. But he was wrong, as far as she was concerned. She hadn't agreed to any of this. And she still had a few days of freedom left before the tour started and Adam became an unwanted presence in her daily life.

She hadn't really lied to him earlier about her plans for the day. She'd simply answered only the question about having to leave to get her dog. That part of it was completely true. Snowball was due to be delivered to her later this evening by one of the doggy day-care staffers. As far as the rest of it, that really wasn't any of his business. Not yet.

She waited several moments after he'd left before returning to her bedroom closet. She slipped off the summer dress and replaced it with her most comfortable pair of jeans and a soft cotton blouse. Pulling her hair up, she secured it in a large tortoise shell clip.

Then she sneaked out of her apartment.

Adam had just finished making some cursory notes outside about Ani's block when he saw a familiar figure exit her building. He watched as she strode confidently to the street and hailed a cab.

What the…? It couldn't have been more than twenty minutes since he'd left her apartment. Where exactly was she going?

Better question was, why hadn't she mentioned her plans to leave?

Was this about a man? She'd been quite hesitant to answer his questions about dating. Perhaps she was going to meet someone right now. But why the secrecy?

Without hesitation, he jogged to his parked car and began to follow her. Every turn took them farther out of greater Dallas. Chic boutiques and swanky restaurants gradually gave way to boarded up buildings and graffiti brick walls. About four miles later, the cab came to a stop.

Adam pulled up behind them and parked his car as Ani exited out the passenger side of the taxi. When she noticed his presence, her surprise quickly collapsed into an expression of clear anger. She stomped her way over to where he stood next to his car.

"What are you doing here?" she demanded.

"I could ask you the same question. I thought you said you weren't going anywhere the rest of the day."

She narrowed her eyes at him. "No. I said nothing of the kind."

Adam pinched the bridge of his nose. Great. Now she was arguing semantics with him. The truth was, she'd deliberately misled him. "You were less than forthcoming."

"Never mind that. Did you just secretly follow me?"

Adam couldn't help a bristle of irritation. She had a lot of nerve stepping out on him like this and then acting as if she was the affronted party. "If it had been a secret, you wouldn't have any idea I was here, sweetheart."

The deep red flush of her cheeks deepened. "Don't call me that!"

Her demand took his ire down a peg. She was right. It was highly unprofessional of him, past history or not. "We should talk about that, by the way," he told her.

"About what, exactly?"

"How you didn't even notice there was a car trailing you all that time. You need to be more aware of your surroundings."

She countered with an exaggerated eye roll. "You had no right to follow me."

"I beg to differ. What are you doing here, anyway?" He glanced up at the sign hanging above the doorway of the gray stone building they stood in front of.

Plano Street Youth Center.

"I hardly see how it's any of your business. Now, if you'll excuse me."

She turned on her heel but Adam stopped her departure with a gentle but firm grip on her elbow. She seared him with a look of outrage.

"Sorry, Ms. Terrance. Not so fast. You may think our association hasn't started yet, but you'd be wrong. It started the moment I left your father's office earlier today after signing a contract. Now please answer the question. What are you doing here?"

She tugged her arm free with so much force, Adam worried for a moment that she might actually topple backward. "See for yourself. If you must." With that, she strode toward the entrance.

Adam released a deep breath and slowly counted to ten. Then he took a moment to pray for patience. He had to make sure to maintain an emotional distance here. The guilt would eat him alive if he failed in his duty yet again.

He followed her inside.

CHAPTER TWO

SHE JUST HAD to get through this trip.

Ani settled into the soft leather seat of the private jet they'd boarded moments before. Adam's jet. He'd insisted they take his private aircraft to Paris rather than follow through with the travel plans the tour management company had made for her. Controlling to the last.

As if she didn't have enough of that in her life.

How hard would it be? She would be plenty busy. Between rehearsing and performing, she had more than enough to keep her mind off her complicated feelings for the man accompanying her. He'd made her so angry, following her to the youth center three days ago. But then he'd sat there patiently for hours while she worked with the kids.

He'd driven her home afterward and mumbled what might be described as an apology, for upsetting her about being followed, explaining that he was only doing his job. He almost sounded conciliatory, regretful. It was a side of him she hadn't really seen before nor expected to see.

Now, she tried not to turn and stare at him behind her. He sat at a round conference table with his crew. Two other men and two women. They appeared to be going over procedure with open blueprint plans of the concert hall spread out in front of them.

It was all so unnecessary. Much ado about nothing.

Moira, her manager and dear friend, approached, providing a much-needed distraction. "You should try to get some rest," she suggested, sitting down in the leather seat next to her.

Like that was possible. Ani's nerves were stretched much too thin thinking about her bodyguard. The fact that she had one still felt like a foreign notion.

"I'll try," she fibbed. "How's Snowball?"

"Resting comfortably in his pen in the back. He seems very unexcited about his trip." She waved a hand at their surroundings. "Not too shabby. This certainly beats flying commercial. Even if we would have been traveling first class. Your fella coming along seems to have its benefits."

"He's certainly not my fella, Moira. Just a friend of my overprotective and paranoid brother. The brother who thinks I'm in unacceptable peril and I need a big, strong crew of babysitters to accompany me on my first trip overseas."

"Well, I'm not going to complain. I'm not sure why you are either." Moira glanced behind them. "That's a whole lot of handsome sitting in one spot."

Ani shrugged. "I haven't really noticed."

Moira rolled her eyes. "That's what I mean. You never notice. Men are staring at you all the time. And you won't give anyone the time of day."

"I don't really have time to give. I would think my manager would appreciate such focus on my craft."

Moira nodded. "Sure I do. But I don't exactly want you to behave like a nun either. There's more to life, you know. When was the last time you even went out on a date?"

Ani sighed. She wasn't really in the mood to

talk about her social life. Or lack thereof. It had been bad enough trying to ditch Adam's questions when he'd been the one asking. "Let's just say my last boyfriend wanted more than I was ready or willing to give." She'd found herself gradually acquiescing to more and more of his requests and increasingly resenting him for it.

"I see," Moira said, as if she hadn't heard the story before. She glanced behind them once more. "But have you ever seen such a gorgeous group?"

One of the men looked up as if sensing Moira's attention. They shared a smile. Moira's cheeks turned pink. Ani had never seen the no-nonsense businesswoman flush before. This might be an interesting trip in more ways than one.

"I think you might need to go get some ice water from the minibar, Moira."

The other woman fanned her face. "Not a bad idea. Can I get you anything?" she asked, standing.

"No, thanks. I'm good."

That description was short-lived. Adam came to sit in the seat only moments after Moira had evacuated it. Would Ani's heart ever stop missing a beat whenever the man approached? He was dressed casually yet professionally in a crisp black T-shirt and pressed khaki pants.

"Ready for takeoff?"

She wasn't ready for any of this. It was hard enough to accept her new reality. She was actually a performing artist with an audience. All the years of hard work and training would finally amount to a career she might be proud of. But it was a demanding one. And now she had the complication of Adam Steele to contend with on top of it all.

"Not really. I'm also not so sure I'm ready for all the rest either," she admitted, surprising herself somewhat. So far, she hadn't actually discussed her anxiety about the mounting pressure of her career with anyone, not even Moira. No, the only way she'd even voiced any of it out loud was during one of the many imaginary conversations she still had with her mother before she began her warm-up whenever she practiced. "It's all a bit scary," she added.

He turned to face her, and for an insane moment, she thought he might actually reach out and touch her. But his hands stayed firmly by his side. "You can feel safe with me. I won't let anyone get near you."

He'd misunderstood. She hadn't been referring to her so-called admirer. Maybe she was being naive about the potential for danger in that respect. But she was so used to Brant and her father blowing things out of proportion where her well-being was concerned.

"It's not that. Not really. I guess I just never stopped to think how overwhelming all of this would feel. Not until it was too late to back out."

Adam studied her face for several beats. "Listen, Ani. You deserve this," he said, surprising her. "You deserve your success. I know you can handle it."

Perhaps he did understand, after all.

He hadn't meant to say all that.

Adam shifted in his seat and wondered why he'd said any of it. His words were too personal. He wasn't here to be Ani's friend—he was here to protect her. His only excuse was that he'd been reading about her over the past couple of days. She was an instant celebrity, totally unprepared for the sudden glare of the spotlight. In interview after interview, she mostly recounted how dreamlike her life had become, how out of place she felt in this new world she found herself in. She wasn't exactly a pop star gracing the pages of music websites, but her pure raw talent and striking good looks had caught the attention of music lovers all over the world.

Another recurring theme in those interviews was how she wished her mother was still around to support her and to celebrate her success.

"Thank you for saying that," she finally replied. "It helps to hear it."

"You're welcome."

The air between them grew awkward. It behooved him to change the subject to less personal matters. "How long have you been volunteering?"

"At the youth center? About three or so years. I performed in a charity event for them, and afterward a lot of the kids came up to say how much they'd enjoyed my playing."

"So you ended up volunteering to provide piano lessons." It didn't surprise him in the least. "That's quite a gift you're giving those kids."

A genuine smile of affection graced her lips. "Those kids give just as much in return. Just watching their hard work and joy from learning to play enriches my life in so many ways."

He wanted to tell her just how much she must mean to those kids. She probably had no clue. He'd spent hours and hours at just such a center as a kid himself. His mother had left when he was barely a teen, and with no father around, he'd been foisted off to live with his aunt and uncle at the age of thirteen. That was when he'd met Brant and all the other kids in that rural town just outside of Dallas, Texas. Most of them were friendly enough, but there were always the snobbish few who kept reminding him that he didn't fit in.

And they were right. He'd never really belonged.

But there was no use in getting into all that with Ani. Again, it was much too personal. She was simply his job for the moment. Nothing more.

So why was he still sitting here next to her when he should be going over more details with his crew? Why did he want to spend the bulk of this flight in this chair chatting with her as they got reacquainted? It made no sense.

But he wanted to know what her life had been like in the years since he'd last seen her. How had the opportunity to play in Paris come about?

Why there was no significant other accompanying her on this trip?

It was a question that he had to eventually ask, from a professional standpoint. He needed to know if a past boyfriend might be behind those mysterious emails. But Adam had to admit his curiosity ran deeper than that. He hadn't stopped thinking about her since the day in her father's office.

That was completely irresponsible and unacceptable. Adam had way too much baggage for the likes of Ani Terrance. He had way too much baggage for anyone. She was a musical talent on the verge of a career most people could only dream about. And she'd already dealt with enough heartbreak and loss in her life.

He had nothing to offer someone like her, couldn't risk the inevitable failure of letting her down as he would most certainly do. Judging by his history.

I can't let you keep holding me back. The feminine voice echoed in his mind as if he were hearing it again this very moment.

"Looks like we're about to take off," he told her, pushing away the wayward memories. "Make yourself comfortable." He stood to leave and go back to join his crew.

"Wait!"

The urgency in her voice gave him pause. "Is something wrong?"

She bit down on her lip. "It's just—I don't fly that often. And I don't seem to see Moira. It's just as the plane lifts off the ground. After that, I should be fine."

"You don't want to be alone at takeoff."

She ducked her head with an embarrassed smile. "It's silly, I know. Once we're in the air, I'm sure I'll be totally fine. I just…need a distraction."

How was he supposed to deny her request? Adam sat back down and the relief in her sigh was clear. "It's not silly, Ani."

"Thanks."

The plane began its taxi journey and Ani's

hands gripped the armrests so tight that her knuckles turned white. He had to resist the urge to reach over and take her hands into his, to try to soothe her anxiety.

"Is this the part where I should distract you?"

She gulped and nodded. "Please."

"Tell me more about the kids you teach. What are they like?"

The tension seemed to melt away from her face. It was replaced with an affectionate, soft expression. "They're so amazing. They each have their challenges with the lot they've been given in life. But none of that seems to have deterred them from reaching for their goals and dreams. They leave me in awe most days."

A sudden sadness appeared in her face as the plane took off. "In many ways, the time I spend with those kids leaves me feeling closer to my own mother." She looked away quickly but not before he caught the slight sheen of tears in her eyes.

"How so?" he prodded, not even caring that they'd somehow broached yet another subject that was much too personal. Why did discussing all this with her feel so natural?

"It just reminds me of all the times I sat beside her as a little girl on the bench while she played." She swiped at her cheeks with the back of her hand. "I like to think she'd be as proud of me as I am of those kids at the center."

Adam couldn't help it. Despite all the reasons to avoid touching her at all costs, this time, he did reach over and take her hand in his.

"I have no doubt of it, Ani. How could she not be?"

So much for keeping her distance from Adam.

Ani couldn't believe what she'd shared with him back on the jet. He'd held her hand. She rubbed her palm over her wrist. She could almost still feel the warmth of his touch.

That tidbit about how volunteering at the center helped her remember her mother wasn't something she'd shared with anyone. Not even her brother or father. And not Moira, who happened to be riding up the hotel elevator with her right now.

They'd arrived in Paris to a beautiful, sunny day. Ani should be elated. She'd always wanted to visit this city. And here she was, under circumstances she would never have dreamed for herself. About to perform for a French audience full of people who'd paid months in advance for the chance to see her.

But all she could think about was the man who'd accompanied her here.

Moira must have somehow read her mind. "You seem off in a distant place," she began as the elevator moved upward. "Any chance you're thinking about a tall, dark-haired body-guard who happened to sit with you for most of the flight here?"

Ani avoided looking at her friend. "I was nervous about flying. He was just being a gentleman, trying to ease my anxiety."

Moira huffed. "That man gives off all sorts of vibes, but gentlemanly is not one of them."

Luckily, the dinging of the elevator spared Ani the need to answer. When they reached her suite, three hotel employees were already there with her luggage, her equipment, and Snowball. The dog perked up in his pen when he saw her, his tail wagging furiously with happiness.

"Look who's awake," Ani cooed, lifting her devoted pet. Her thank-you was a flurry of sandpaper-tongue licks. "You were a good boy on the plane. Yes, you were. Who's my good boy?"

Moira giggled at the spectacle, no doubt because of the exaggerated voice Ani was using to greet her pup.

The sound of someone clearing their throat behind them had Ani halting midnuzzle. She could just guess who it was standing in the doorway. The throat clearing was quickly followed by an all-too-familiar masculine voice: "Hello."

Ani quickly put Snowball back in his crate, to the animal's deep upset judging by his immediate yelping.

"Uh, hi. I was just…saying hi to my dog."

Moira giggled again. Ani resisted the urge to give her friend a small nudge.

"Can I come in?" Adam asked, still standing in the doorway.

Ani nodded.

"I just want to take a quick look at the room, check out the locks, that sort of thing." Adam strode into the suite with his usual air of authority. She could have sworn she saw one of the bellhops give a small bow at his entrance.

"Sure thing."

"I was just leaving," Moira announced and

followed the hotel employees out the door. She firmly shut it closed behind her.

Traitor.

Ani swallowed the ball of apprehension lodged in her throat. It was one thing to sit side by side with Adam in a jet full of others. But being alone with him always seemed to throw her off balance. And now they were alone in a luxurious hotel room overlooking the Seine. She wondered how many couples must have honeymooned in this very suite. Her mind brought up all sorts of unwanted images, all of them starring a very sexy and brooding bodyguard who happened to be staring at her dog at the moment.

"What's that?" he asked, pointing to where Snowball sat still whining in his crate.

"*That* is my dog. Snowball."

Adam looked over at her and crossed his arms in front of his chest. "You are a liar, Ms. Terrance."

Ani bit back a gasp. "What's that supposed to mean?"

"That is clearly a rabbit or hare of some sort."

It was only then that she noticed the tiniest tug of a smile around his lips. She thrust her hands on her hips in mock offense. "You must apologize to my fierce and loyal guard dog at once."

"You mean your guard bunny?" He pointed down at Snowball once more. "Look at those ears. Only bunny rabbits have ears that long and pointy. And he's as cottony white as any rabbit I've ever seen."

"Well, I never." Ani leaned down and picked up her dog. "We don't have to listen to this, do we, Snowball?" She made an exaggerated show of walking away.

Only, Snowball had other plans. He practically leaped out of her arms toward Adam.

Adam caught the animal just in time. Impressive reflexes, though she shouldn't be surprised. It was Adam's turn to be on the receiving end of wet doggy kisses.

"*Et tu*, Snowball?" How many traitors were in her orbit, anyway?

"Oh, yeah. He's definitely fierce, all right," Adam said in a muffled voice as he unsuccessfully tried to duck from all the canine kisses.

Ani couldn't hold back the laughter any longer. Come to think of it, she couldn't quite recall the last time she'd so much as giggled, let alone indulged in a good, hearty belly laugh, what with the pressure of the tour, the stress of knowing her brother and father were so worried about her and the sorrow of missing her mother during such a momentous time in her life. But somehow, in this moment, she was finally enjoying some humor.

She threw a glance at Adam who was now playfully nuzzling the dog, and had to admit what she didn't want to face. He was the reason she was finally enjoying herself.

The last time Adam had interacted with a dog, it was a German shepherd trained to sniff out explosives. He hardly knew what to do with one this small and…energetic.

"Looks like you made a new friend," Ani said after a steady stream of laughter.

He set down the dog and studied her. "I really hope so, kitten."

The amusement dropped away in an instant. So she remembered; he saw it on her facial expression.

He hadn't meant to call her by the name he'd used for her all those years ago when they were both kids. Back then, he'd been mocking her.

He'd been all kinds of a jerk as a teen. Mostly to cover up the hurt and embarrassment of his existence. Unfortunately, Ani had been one of his targets.

What kind of name is that? Anikita? I can't pronounce that. I'll just call you kitty. Or kitten. Or maybe kitty cat.

He ducked his head with embarrassment at the memory. "Listen, I was kind of a jerk to you when we were younger. I should apologize for that."

"No apology necessary. It was a long time ago."

"Maybe. But I shouldn't have been such an—"

She held her hand up to stop him before he could continue.

"I guess I took it as some sort of compliment." She looked away as a pink flush crept into her cheeks. "You didn't seem to have any kind of nickname for anyone else. It was almost a term of endearment as far as I was concerned. Silly, I know."

Adam reached over to run a finger down her cheek. He couldn't seem to eradicate this strong urge to touch her. "Only thing silly about it is that you apparently gave me way too much credit. You should have given me a hard smack across the forehead."

She snorted. "As if. You were much bigger than me. I wouldn't have risked the potential retaliation."

Adam felt the color drain from his face. He prayed she was joking. A tremor of horror traveled up his spine. She couldn't have ever thought that way about him, ever thought that he might strike her or any other woman for that matter.

It was bad enough that his error in judgment had caused such injury and suffering. He would never get over the guilt. An image of Tonya's bruised and damaged body assaulted his mind, and his blood ran cold.

"Are you okay?" Ani asked, as if sensing his discomfort. Her eyes held his for countless moments. Neither one seemed able to move. He thought he might have stopped breathing.

"I would never have so much as touched you, kitten. Not under any circumstances."

A knock sounded on the door before he could say any more.

Ani didn't tear her gaze away from his. "I

should get that," she announced, but stood still where she was. As if waiting for him to concur.

He was about to tell her to ignore it, that they had some things to discuss. But the knock came again, louder this time.

Ani studied him a second longer before releasing a deep sigh. She turned away to get the door.

He finally came to his senses and stopped her with a gentle grip on her elbow. "Let me."

A look through the peephole revealed a well-heeled, tall man in a designer suit and hair slicked back within an inch of its survival. A pair of piercing blue eyes and angular cheekbones rounded out the look of a native Parisian son.

"Were you expecting someone?" Adam asked Ani over his shoulder.

"I was told someone from the theater might stop by upon my arrival. Just to go over some things."

Adam opened the door a few inches.

"Bonjour," the man said with a smile. "My name is Philippe Penault. I'm here to see Mademoiselle Terrance. I'm with the Le Trianon theater," he added with a thick French accent.

There was no doubt the man was exactly who he said he was. Adam stepped aside to let him in. Philippe didn't hesitate to make a beeline to Ani and landed a small peck to the back of her hand.

Adam watched as the two exchanged introductions and pleasantries. The man was the epitome of sophistication and elegant charm. Qualities Adam would never hope to have. Something tightened in his gut as he watched Ani smile at the stranger, displaying a rudimentary knowledge of French. He knew a bit himself, having owned property in France for the past several years now.

Still, he felt a bit like the help watching his employer with a guest. Which was essentially an accurate description...

No matter how much money he had now or how successful he'd become professionally, Adam knew when he didn't fit in. Just as he hadn't as a kid in that tiny little town he and Ani had grown up in.

Now, Philippe was asking Ani to accompany him to a nearby café to discuss her upcoming performance in his theater. Adam interrupted before she could answer.

"I don't think that's a good idea," he declared in English. There was no way he was letting Ani out of his sight in this city. And somehow, he didn't think he'd be extended an invitation by Philippe.

Ani's jaw dropped. "Why ever not?"

Adam crossed his arms in front of his chest, bracing for the argument sure to follow. What kind of question was that? Didn't she know he had a job to do? He was in charge of her security detail. That responsibility included things like not letting her wander around an unfamiliar city with a man she'd literally just met.

His irritation had nothing to do with how handsome this Philippe was. Nor the way he was looking at Ani as if she were a delicate piece of pastry he couldn't wait to get alone to himself.

Jealousy had nothing to do with it, he reassured the nagging voice in his head. He was simply doing his job.

Adam spoke French. Maybe not fluently, but enough to hold a pretty steady conversation with the rep from the theater. Ani glanced at him now sitting at a nearby table scrolling on his smartphone. They'd agreed to head to a nearby sidewalk café. She and Philippe sat alone going over some of the details about her performance tomorrow night. Adam's eyes may have been on his screen but Ani had no doubt his attention was laser focused on her.

She'd stood and watched with her mouth agape back in the hotel room as he'd explained to Philippe, mostly in French, that he was in charge of her security and he wasn't about to let her out of his sight. He certainly hadn't asked her for any say in the matter.

She wasn't sure whether to be furious, embarrassed or downright impressed with his communication skills. The man was a constant source of surprise. And a frequent source of pure, unfiltered frustration.

Focus. Ani forced her attention back to the tablet Philippe had set down on the table between them. They were going over last-minute details to ensure a smooth performance, hopefully resulting in glowing reviews. She appreciated that the venue was going the extra mile to ensure she had a successful night. This was her career, after all. At the least, she owed this man her full, undistracted attention. But her gaze seemed to constantly drift to her dark, brooding bodyguard who sat a few feet away.

Several of the tables around them were occupied by couples who appeared completely enamored with each other. Old and young alike. Paris certainly seemed to be the city of love as reputed. Many of them held hands. One couple kept feeding each other pieces of cake.

It had never occurred to Ani before that she wanted that experience with someone. She wanted to sit at a romantic café by the Seine as the lights slowly flickered on around the city with the Eiffel Tower looming like a majestic steel mountain in the distance. She wanted to have her lover offer her a piece of his fruit crepe, then slowly wipe her lips with his napkin. Afterward, they would hold hands as they entered their small apartment. Then later they would indulge in a night full of passion in each other's arms.

Ani reached for her sparkling wine and took a long sip.

Heaven help her, Adam was the man she was imagining in all those scenarios. Though he hardly seemed the type to delicately feed a woman cake. In fact, the very notion was almost laughable.

An audible giggle actually escaped her lips. Adam even looked up, gave her what could only be described as a glare.

What was wrong with him? What did he have against amusement, anyway? He'd seemed happy enough when she was laughing about Snowball back in the hotel room when they'd been alone.

She looked up to find Philippe studying her questioningly. *"Pardon,* mademoiselle," he began in French before adding in accented English, "You appear a bit distracted. Is everything all right?"

Ani wanted to kick herself. This was her career, for heaven's sake. Damn Adam Steele for the way he was distracting her from something so important.

"I'm so sorry, Philippe. I don't mean to drift off."

He gave her a charming smile. "But it is I who should be sorry. You must be exhausted after your long day of travel." He powered off the tablet. "That is enough for now. I have no doubt you'll be magnificent tomorrow night.

Please call if you need anything in the mean-time."

The man had barely pulled his chair back when Adam materialized by their table. He was certainly fast on his feet. Yet another talent.

"Finished?"

"Oui," Philippe answered. "Do you two know your way back to the hotel?"

"We'll manage." Adam sounded somewhat dismissive and needlessly curt. What was his problem all of a sudden? They seemed to have had a minor truce starting during the flight and then later in the suite with Snowball. He'd even called her kitten and apologized for giving her the nickname to begin with. Now he was act-ing surly and annoyed all over again.

She'd had very little experience with the op-posite sex. As intrusive and overprotective as her father and brother were, most of her boy-friends were either scared off before things turned serious or she wasn't interested enough to invest in the effort her family would put her through. The closest thing she'd ever had to a boyfriend had been a selfish and demanding oil heir unwilling to compromise in the slightest way. Besides, her exhaustive practice schedule and long daily lessons left very little time for a social life.

It wasn't as if she was some virginal maiden. But her realm of experience was vastly limited. She may have been intimate with a man in the past, but she'd never actually felt close to one. She simply didn't have the necessary skill set to try to decipher a man like Adam.

She just hated that she wanted to try so badly.

Philippe glanced between Adam and Ani, still seated in her chair. "Might I suggest walking along the river to get back? This time of evening, it's quite romantic."

Was it her imagination or had he emphasized the last word unnecessarily? Dropping a small peck on her cheek, he gave Adam a small nod before walking away.

One thing was certain, Adam wouldn't be at all interested in any type of stroll, particularly a romantic one along the Seine. She glanced at the walkway leading to the riverbank with abject longing and sighed. Maybe tomorrow morning she could bring Snowball here and take him on a nice, long walk. Who needed a man when she had her trusted canine companion?

But he surprised her yet again with his next words.

"I could use some fresh air and exercise." He extended his hand. "I say we take Philippe up on his suggestion."

It took a moment for the words to register in her brain, for her to convince herself that she'd actually heard him correctly. Wordlessly, she placed her fingers in his open palm over the table. Still, she couldn't seem to get her legs to work and stand up until Adam gave her hand a small tug.

"What do you say, kitten? Come walk with me."

CHAPTER THREE

"ACTUALLY, I'VE CHANGED my mind."

Adam's announcement as they reached the riverbank had Ani halting in her tracks. She knew it! Whatever had compelled him to suggest going on this stroll with her, he'd up and changed his mind. Nothing like getting a girl's hopes up. He really did have whiplash-inducing mood swings.

She bit down on her frustration and tried to settle the tide of anger threatening to burst through the surface of her calm facade. When was she going to get a chance like this again? She liked to think she'd get another opportunity to come back to Paris. To sit in another café, maybe even with a man. To walk with him as they took in the beautiful sight of Paris in the evening.

But she wanted that experience here and now. Even if the man currently present was only here as a favor to her brother, who was paying him to keep an eye on her.

"Fine," she bit out, turning on her heel to walk back to the hotel.

"Whoa." Adam stopped her with a touch at the small of her back. Even in her ire, she felt the electricity through the thin fabric of her dress.

"Where are you going?" he asked.

"Back to the hotel. You said you changed your mind."

He smiled at her, a twinkle of mischief in his eye. "Just about the walk."

Well, that was something of a relief. She eyed a nearby park bench. He didn't seem the type to sit around and people watch for fun. But what did she really know?

"Hang on a second," he ordered, then stepped a few feet away. She watched as he made a phone call and proceeded to converse in French with whoever was on the other line. When he was done, he came over to her once more.

"Here, let's go." He guided her along, again with the hand at her back just above the waist. The contact was wreaking havoc with her emotions.

"Where are we going?"

"You'll see."

A minute or so later, they approached a docked, glass-covered canopy boat. She could see a number of tables on board topped with white linen cloths and lit candles.

"It occurred to me neither of us really had a chance to have dinner."

She couldn't seem to summon the words as he guided her to the vessel and helped her on board.

"Uh…you arranged for a dinner cruise? Right there on the pathway?"

He shrugged. "I have a few contacts in the city. We can do something else if you're not up for it."

Was he serious? She'd have to be daft to turn this opportunity down. She told him as much.

A tuxedoed crew member greeted them and led them to a table. The glass canopy made for an amazing view and they hadn't even left the dock yet. Ani had to bite back her excitement. This was so unexpected. A girl could get used to such surprises.

Oh, yeah. Despite his tendency to frequently and consistently heighten her emotions, Ani figured she could get used to Adam Steele in all manner of ways.

A sommelier appeared before she'd even had a chance to fully be seated. The woman greeted them with a smile and popped open a chilled bottle of champagne. At Adam's nod, the smiling woman started to pour the bubbly liquid into two tall glass flutes.

Adam lifted his glass as soon as the sommelier walked away. "A toast to your upcoming performance."

"Thank you." Ani clinked her glass to his and took a small sip. The buttery, crisp taste exploded on her tongue. It was exquisite, a burst of flavor filling her mouth and running over her tongue.

Her senses were in overdrive. Watching scene after charming scene as they floated along the river, the taste of the rich champagne and the lure of the man sitting across from her made for a heady mixture of emotion.

Ani watched in awe as the boat passed a group of young adults dancing along the river's edge. The Eiffel Tower stood majestically in the distance, breathtakingly lit up.

"I couldn't have imagined a better way to

spend the evening, Adam. I don't know how I'll be able to repay you for this."

He gave her a smile that made her stomach do a little flip. "No need. I'm glad you're enjoying yourself."

She didn't get a chance to respond as yet another server appeared with two salads. Or maybe salad wasn't the right word. On her plate sat a work of art—a romaine leaf topped with perfectly cubed avocado and bright red sliced tomato surrounded by a smattering of exotic-looking herbs laid out in an eye-pleasing design. Ani fought hard to resist the urge to pull out her phone and take a photo. That would look less than sophisticated in such a setting. She didn't want to appear like the awestruck tourist that she was.

The main course was a seared fish fillet topped with a drizzle of zesty plum sauce. It was followed by an airy dessert of fruit-topped macarons that practically melted in her mouth.

"This is perfect," she announced, stabbing a fork into a plump slice of strawberry. "I don't like to eat too heavy before a performance day. This was the ideal meal, light and delicious."

"Glad to hear it."

Ani leaned back to take in the breathtaking view of the riverside as their plates were cleared and the interior lights dimmed even further.

"You speak French," she ventured at last.

He gave a small shrug. "It was my assigned language class in school. Picked it up some more during a couple tours overseas. Then when I bought property out here, it was pretty much immersion learning."

Ani knew she was being silly, but she couldn't help the feeling of inadequacy that washed over her. Adam was worldly, successful and knowledgeable. By contrast, most of her life had been spent honing her musical skills and trying to pick up the pieces of her shattered family after their tragic loss.

"You look like you traveled a thousand miles in your head just now," Adam told her with a small smile.

She hadn't meant to drift off. "I was just admiring the city. It's taking my breath away."

"First time in Paris will have that effect. I take it you haven't been here before."

She shook her head. "No."

"I must say I'm a little surprised. Considering… Never mind."

She knew what he'd been about to say. Her family had certainly had the means. Not only did her father come from money, he'd inherited a successful business and grown it. Of course, there'd been opportunities to travel. She just hadn't wanted to leave home. Not until her father had somehow finished grieving. Only, he never really had.

"I would have loved to," she admitted. "Just didn't ever really get a chance."

Not with a father and older brother to look after. Brant himself had been in no condition to lend any kind of emotional support to their grieving parent. She either had to step up or watch her father withdraw further from the world and life in general.

"Why is that?" Adam probed.

Surprisingly, she didn't find herself annoyed by the question. This wasn't a topic she normally opened up about. But for some reason, it felt natural to do so with Adam. Probably because she'd known him as a child. What other reason could there be?

"My father needed me around," she found herself explaining. "So did Brant. Neither were interested in taking any kind of vacation. Dad sort of immersed himself in his work." And Brant had withdrawn.

"Sounds like you took on a lot at a young age."

"I had to." She sucked in a deep breath. "The thing about having a devoted and loving parent is the unbearable depth of grief that results from their loss." She studied her fingernails. She'd never said as much out loud before. Despite living with those exact thoughts every single day.

Adam was quiet for a long while before he finally spoke. "I guess I wouldn't know."

Ani found herself asking the question she'd wondered about for the past several years, ever since she'd first met him. "How did you come to live with your aunt and uncle?"

Another shrug. "No big mystery. My old man just left one day. And my mother split soon after."

She didn't have the words to respond to that— the concept was so incomprehensible. Despite the unbearable pain, she'd been lucky to have her mom for the short amount of time Ani had been given with her.

A strange yet comfortable silence ensued

between them until Adam finally broke it. "Should I order another bottle of champagne?"

"Absolutely not. Not for me, anyway." As tempted as she was by the offer, she did have to perform tomorrow. Bubbly that good was easy to overindulge in. Not to mention, she didn't want to risk too much of a drop in her inhibitions around this man. She had already confided much more than she had ever intended to.

Although, he seemed to have confided as well. She couldn't be too cross with herself. She could chalk it up to two old friends simply catching up. Though her feelings for him were starting to edge out of friendship boundaries.

"In that case, let's go above deck," he suggested. "We're approaching the Eiffel Tower. We can watch it from the outside."

He walked around the table and pulled her chair out. Once more, she felt his hand at the small of her back as he guided her above deck. He had no idea what that intimate touch did to her insides. Probably because he didn't view it as intimate at all. He probably wouldn't give it a second thought. Whereas she felt warmth resonate from his hand and travel all the way down to her toes.

* * *

He wasn't usually an impulsive man. In fact, he was characteristically calm and controlled. Every minute of his day was typically planned out. Tonight, he was supposed to have gone back to his hotel room, gone over some more details about the layout of the theater with his crew and then answered some emails. Afterward, he'd planned to work on a bid for an expansion of his firm into the Eastern European market. But then Philippe had mentioned a stroll along the riverbank and Ani's eyes had taken on a wistful look at the suggestion.

Admittedly, he had taken things to a whole other level by arranging for a dinner cruise for the two of them. He couldn't even explain it to himself.

Not that he regretted it. And therein was the real kicker. It was a beautiful night. Paris, as usual, didn't disappoint. He was glad to be out here, watching the sights of this dynamic, historic city with Ani Terrance.

She sighed next to him as they leaned over the railing, watching as the Eiffel Tower approached. "My kids would love to see this. I'm going to try to find a way to fund a trip when I get back."

"They mean a lot to you, don't they? The kids you teach."

Her features softened as she smiled. "They're family. Particularly the girls. Like the sisters I never had. I like to think they view me the same way." She chuckled. "I know that must sound silly. I'm only there to teach them piano. Not for some deep, intense connection."

He instinctively stepped closer to her. The barest brush of his shoulder against her arm. "It doesn't sound silly at all. The people I count as my family aren't blood relatives at all."

"Oh? What about your aunt and uncle?"

Adam felt the familiar churning in his gut at yet another mention of his so-called kin. "I'll always feel grateful to them for taking me in. But we're not particularly close." Aunt Rose and Uncle Stan had been dutiful enough to fulfill their responsibility. But it had been hard to ignore, all those years, their reluctance to have an unwanted teenager thrust into their lives.

Ani didn't press when he said no more. Thankfully.

"Yeah. My 'family,' quote unquote, include the crew back at the hotel, the men I served with, including your brother. A handful of others I've been fortunate enough to have enter into my life," he told her.

She bit her top lip with her lower teeth. "And a girlfriend, I imagine." She'd barely gotten the last word out when her hand flew to her mouth. "I'm sorry. I don't know where that came from. It's really none of my business."

"It's all right."

"I'm just not very good at making conversation."

He felt oddly disappointed in her explanation.

"Well, the answer happens to be that there is no girlfriend. I'm not in one place long enough."

"I see."

"What about you? You never really answered my questions back at the apartment about any men in your life."

She huffed out a small laugh. "I recall you wanting names."

He chuckled at that.

She ducked her head, looked down toward the water. "Are you asking as my bodyguard now? Or would you personally like to know?"

He shrugged. They were in dangerous territory here. He knew he should answer the question the only way that a professional would. But he couldn't seem to stop himself when the right words did not come out of his mouth. "Maybe I'm just making conversation too."

She looked away with a slight smile. "But you're not. You're asking because it's your job."

The truth was, Adam couldn't even be sure anymore. The lines were becoming increasingly blurred. Which was completely unacceptable. He knew all too well the danger of blurring such lines. The risks could be tragic and near deadly. Memories assaulted him before he could push them away. Memories of a deafening explosion, followed by a surreal quiet, then nothing but smoke and fire.

"So, what's your answer then?" he prompted, forcing himself to focus.

She sighed deeply before shaking her head. "No. I have no name to give you. And I'm not much of a social media or online type of girl. I spend way too much time at a different kind of keyboard. So no dating sites. I find myself very single currently."

Currently. "And before? There has to be

someone in your past. I'm afraid I have to look at every possibility, Ani."

She shut her eyes. "The only person who even came close was a man named Peter Myer. But he was the one who walked away. Wanted much more than I was willing or ready to commit to."

Adam made a mental note of the name. He would do some research on this Peter later. He already felt an inexplicable, intense dislike for the man. A man he'd never met.

"Peter Myer is a fool," he spat out, before he thought better of it.

She turned to him, gasping in surprise. "Come again?"

No turning back now. "Only a fool would walk away from you, Ani. You're attractive in all manner of ways. I've always thought so," he found himself admitting, simply because he wanted to get it off his chest. Plus, he figured she deserved to hear the truth after all these years. Clearly, the mood and the magic of Paris had gone to his head. "Since we were teens."

She stared at him with her mouth agape. "You what?"

"You had to have suspected."

She guffawed. "No, Adam. I didn't. After all, you looked utterly disgusted every time I tried to talk to you when you came by to visit Brant. You left the pool if I so much as dipped a toe in it. You canceled plans to go to the movies or to a party if Brant agreed to bring me along. In fact, I got the impression you couldn't stand me."

"I tried very hard to have you believe that."

She pulled her hair off her forehead. "But why? Why did you act like you thought I was a pest all those times?"

Adam sighed. He hadn't realized his efforts all those years ago had been quite so successful. A twinge of guilt settled in his chest. "Self-preservation, kitten. I had to save face."

"Save face? I don't understand. What exactly were you thinking?" She seemed genuinely confused.

"Aside from you being the baby sister of one of my closest friends? Or how about the fact that you were way out of my league? The cherished daughter of a prominent Dallas family while I was a castoff nobody wanted. That's what I was thinking."

"You were so much more than that."

He didn't know how to respond to that. A long silence ensued. He'd shocked her. Well, he was a little surprised himself. At no point during the evening had he ever intended to get into all the ways he'd felt for her as a teen.

Time to change the subject. He pointed to the leather clutch she held. "Give me your phone. You want to snap some photos and take some videos to show the kids at the center, don't you?"

Ani gave a visible shake of her head as if to clear it. Then glanced at the scenery behind her. "Yes. I absolutely do."

Adam had just started taking snapshots with the Eiffel Tower behind her when they were approached by another couple.

"We'd be happy to take one of the two of you," the woman said in perfect English, smiling. "Shame not to get one with you both in it. You're such a lovely couple."

"Oh, we're not—he's just—" Ani stammered. But the woman wasn't really listening as she reached for the phone in Adam's hand.

Adam didn't bother to correct her. He stood next to Ani and smiled for the photo. Before long, all four of them were posing together, the City of Lights a stunning background behind them.

"I might not ever forgive you for this," Moira announced dramatically when Ani made it back to her hotel room. Ani knew her well enough to know she was simply teasing. About what, she couldn't guess.

"I apologize profusely, Moira. But what transgression might I have committed unknowingly?"

"Really? You can't guess?"

Ani simply shrugged. Snowball trotted over and dropped at her feet.

Moira uncurled herself from her seat on the plush leather sofa. A black-and-white movie was playing on the TV, English captions scrolling at the bottom of the screen.

"Aside from a text asking if I'd watch Snowball for the evening, you didn't offer one clue about where you were. Just that you would be walking along the Seine."

"And you wanted more detail than that?"

"Of course," Moira answered, a smile tugging at the corners of her mouth. "Especially since you left with that sexy bodyguard of yours, so I have to assume you two have been together all this time."

Ani kicked her shoes off and headed toward the minibar. She needed a tall, cold bottle of water after all the authentic champagne she'd indulged in. "Again. I apologize, Moira. And thank you for keeping an eye on Snowball for me."

"Anytime. I love that big fluff ball of a dog."

"Still, I owe you."

Moira waved that off. "The only thing you owe me is a detailed account of exactly what the two of you were doing. You were out and about in the city of lovers, after all."

Ani uncapped a large bottle of mineral water and took a long sip before answering. "It wasn't like that. He's been here before and Philippe from the theater suggested we enjoy the walk along the riverbank. There's so much happening there. Everything from dancing to floating cafés to sidewalk performers."

"So is that what you did? Walk along the river? You were gone an awful long time."

Ani swallowed some more water. "At first.

Then Adam was nice enough to treat me to a river cruise to sightsee farther along the river."

Moira clapped her hands in front of her face. "Oh, did he now? Tell me everything!"

Ani rubbed a hand across her forehead. "I will. I promise. But can it wait?"

Disappointment washed over Moira's face.

"It's just that I should really go get cleaned up and try to get a good night's sleep before the big day."

Her friend sighed. "I suppose. But right after the performance, you and I are going to sit down while you indulge me in a complete tell-all about your evening."

Ani landed a small peck on her cheek. "It's a deal."

She turned and walked out of the room before Moira could come up with a way to protest the agreement.

In the bathroom, Ani leaned over the sink and studied her face in the wall-to-wall mirror. A large Jacuzzi-style tub of Italian marble called to her, but she did need to get to bed. As it was, she doubted she'd fall asleep anytime soon. Not with the thoughts of the previous few hours running through her head.

She couldn't read too much into the moments she'd just shared with Adam. Aside from their past history, they had nothing in common. And the only thing she should be thinking about right now was her concert tomorrow night.

Still, she'd be lying if she'd said his admission back on the boat didn't make her nearly giddy inside. He'd been attracted to her when they'd been younger. He found her attractive now. The knowledge sent a surge of excitement through her core.

She filled the stainless steel sink, poured a few drops of essential oil in, then soaked both her hands in the warm water. She couldn't risk any inflammation in her finger joints. As much as she'd enjoyed tonight, it probably hadn't been a good idea to stay out.

No one should be distracting her this much. Let alone a man so far out of her reach. Despite his admission, in the end, his words didn't actually change anything. There couldn't be anything real between the two of them. He'd told her earlier he never even stayed in one location long enough to establish any kind of real relationship. Meanwhile, this was her first international trip.

This was not a time in her life to even entertain the notion of any kind of relationship. Her career was finally on the verge of a major milestone. If this mini tour proved profitable for the venues booking her, she could prove herself to the international music community and achieve a level of success most musicians only dreamed of. She'd show that she could drive ticket sales.

And anyway, she had more than her share of overbearing, powerful men in her life. The last thing she needed was a romantic relationship with a man like that. This tour was finally a chance for her to experience some true power and control of her own. She knew her father and brother both loved her dearly and that they meant well, but it was hard not to feel suffocated at times.

Things would be so much different if her mother were alive. The light had gone out of all three of their lives when they'd lost her. Her father had never really summoned a genuine smile after. The sadness never left his eyes.

Therein lay another reason she had no desire

to pursue any kind of relationship. She'd seen firsthand and up close how completely shattered her father was after the loss of his wife. Zini Terrance had been taken away from them much too soon. Her father still hadn't recovered. Years of therapy had helped, but the man was a broken shell of the person he'd been previously. Her parents may have shared a love for the ages, but it had resulted in utter tragedy for them both. Ani had vowed as a teen to never leave herself that vulnerable to loss. It simply couldn't be worth the pain.

There was no reason to revisit that vow. Adam Steele was a temporary flash in her life. After this mini tour, she may not even see him again. An ache settled in her chest at the thought, right in the vicinity of her heart.

Ani leaned her forehead against the mirror and tried for a steadying breath.

She'd been woefully unprepared to have Adam Steele reenter her life.

It was barely dawn, but Adam figured he may as well get out of bed. Not like he'd slept much, anyway. A set of dark, almond-shaped eyes had been there to greet him every time he'd so much as closed his eyes. When he did fall asleep, dreams of an angelic face surrounded by fiery red hair had haunted him throughout the night.

Throwing on a pair of shorts and a T-shirt, he made his way downstairs and out into the street for an early morning run. Hopefully, it would help to clear his head.

Going out with Ani last night had been a mistake. He'd tried to tell himself he'd simply be spending a few hours catching up with an old friend. That it would be a crime to have her miss the beauty of this city her first time here by holing up in her hotel room and practicing piano. But by the time they'd made it back up the elevator, he was thinking of her as much more than a friendly acquaintance from the past.

He had to put an end to that. And fast.

Adam broke into a fast jog as soon as he hit the pavement. Inviting her on that dinner cruise had been reckless and impulsive on his part. He simply should have taken Ani on the scenic route back to their hotel. Hell, he could have even arranged the dinner cruise for her and her friend slash manager instead. In hindsight, that would have been the better plan.

A woman like Ani was off-limits. Completely taboo.

He was older than her, not by a long stretch, but years weren't the only measurement for a life. She was a relative innocent. He'd been a soldier who'd served in some of the most nightmarish, war-torn areas of the world. The ugliness he'd witnessed, the darkness of humanity he'd been privy to, would affect him for the rest of his life. Before that, he'd been an orphaned and unwanted kid who'd repeatedly found himself in trouble.

He'd done well for himself since those younger days. But he'd long ago accepted that he wasn't the type to settle down and commit.

No, he was much better suited to a life of constant change and travel. A life in which he kept the darkness all to himself. Where he could keep his mistakes from hurting anyone else.

Then there was the complication of Ani being the adored baby sister of one of his closest friends. Things didn't get more complicated than that.

Adam set a punishing pace as he made his

way down the streets. Around him, Paris was mostly still asleep. A few of the cafés had the lights turned on low, one or two people stirring about inside. He ran by a bakery and the enticing aroma of fresh baked bread had him slowing his stride.

It occurred to him that Ani would never have experienced tasting a fresh-baked baguette straight from a Parisian oven. Maybe he should pick up a loaf for her on the way back. Along with some sweet cream butter. He imagined feeding her a piece the way those couples were feeding each other cake at the café yesterday.

Just. Stop.

Adam ran a few more steps and then stopped to lean against the wall of a fashion boutique. That was it. No more excuses. He had to stop thinking about her. From now on, he'd be nothing more than the man in charge of her security detail. He'd assign April or Tito to take the lead in communicating with the VIP.

That was the way he had to think of Ani from now. Merely another client he'd been hired to serve.

Strictly professional. Even if it meant he had to stay the hell away from her.

* * *

Ani awoke to find a text message on her phone.

Please notify me when you're up. We have some details to go over. Also, I have something to give you.

It was from April. Ani had met her on the jet, one of the professionals on Adam's security team. Ani responded to have her come up in twenty minutes after she had a chance to shower.

There was a knock on her door exactly twenty minutes later. Ani opened the door to find April standing in the hallway. She held a large brown bag. A delicious aroma wafted into the room and immediately made Ani's mouth water.

She stepped aside to let the other woman in.

April handed her the bag. "This is for you and your team. Various pastries and a fresh baguette. There's even a treat for the dog. From Adam."

Ani managed to mutter a thank-you through her surprise. A touching warmth spread throughout her chest. He'd thought to get her breakfast.

But why was it April who was delivering it?

Adam had mentioned he'd stop by in the morning to brief her about where exactly his men would be positioned during her performance and how she'd be accompanied to and from the stage. Why was April the one here instead?

It should have been a relief. Hadn't she just resolved to herself last night that she had to keep herself guarded as far as he was concerned?

But she couldn't stop wondering about the answer. Though she couldn't bring herself to ask.

CHAPTER FOUR

ADAM OBSERVED THE growing crowd around the theater. A lot of people were here early, as soon as the doors opened. The makeup of the concertgoers surprised him. Elderly groups, several young adults. Even several teens. Ani attracted a very diverse crowd. It had to say something about her talent that her music appealed to such a wide audience.

Something akin to pride blossomed in his chest. Though that was downright silly. He had no right to any such feeling where she was concerned.

He'd avoided her most of the day, aside from a couple of quick, face-to-face checks and text messages. He'd put April in charge of most of the day's responsibilities that involved direct VIP contact.

Far from making him feel better, he'd been miserable and surly, even snapping at his crew more than once.

A buzz sounded in his ear, followed by April's voice. "VIP limo approaching. ETA three mins."

Adam clicked the earpiece. "Cleared for arrival. Side entrance as planned."

"Copy."

Two and a half minutes later, a sleek dark limousine turned around the street corner. Adam scanned the area; the crowd seemed to be contained in front of the box office doors at the front of the theater. A few wanderers here and there paid no mind to the limousine or the two black SUVs that followed. Two of his men were positioned inside, along with the theater's own security crew. April was in the limo with Ani. The performance was due to begin in a couple of hours.

The convoy pulled to a stop at the curb and the limo door opened. April got out first and held the door open for Ani and Moira. Then Ani exited the vehicle, and the sight nearly took his breath away.

She was dressed in a long satin gown the color of the midnight sky over the Mediterranean Sea. Strapless, it exposed her elegant shoulders and long, bare neck. Her hair was done up in a complicated style with delicate ringlets framing her face. She looked like the budding international music star that she was. Someone on the brink of a rich, full life filled with achievement.

Someone he had no business coveting in any way.

He watched as she stepped out onto the curb. Her gaze immediately found him and she gave him a small smile. Yet even from this distance, he could see the confusion clouding her eyes, perhaps wondering why he'd been so unavailable all day. He'd simply been trying to remain at a professional distance. What he should have done all along.

Now, he gave her a nod and an appreciative wink, professionalism be damned. Her smile grew wider. But then April gently nudged her toward the entrance of the building, with Moira trailing closely behind.

He waited a few more moments to ensure nothing or no one suspicious appeared before entering the building himself.

Her dressing room was clearly marked with a gold, glittering star on the door. He could hear voices and the bustle of movement inside.

A soundtrack of classical music played in the background. A piano concerto.

He forced himself to walk past and down the hallway without knocking. There was no real need to check on her. April had things well under control. The stage had been secured several times throughout the day. Nothing had been left to chance.

So why did he feel so out of sorts?

An hour and a half went by as the auditorium gradually grew noisier. Adam watched from behind the large red curtain as every seat eventually filled. She'd sold out the house.

Finally, a hush settled over the crowd as the curtains drew apart. The lights flickered twice before dimming. Ani walked slowly onstage to loud applause.

Once again, her gaze made a straight beeline to where he stood off to the side. Even from here, he could sense her nervousness. He gave her what he hoped was a reassuring smile, one she returned with tight lips.

She turned back to the crowd.

"Bonjour!" she began, and then added in flawless French, "I'm so happy to be here to-

night. Thank you for inviting me to your enchanting city."

Her audience clapped and cheered in response. With a small wave, she took a seat at the grand piano in the center of the stage. The orchestra section darkened.

She began to play.

The sheer beauty of it stunned Adam where he stood. He'd never particularly been a fan of the classics. But there was no doubt he was witnessing creative magic as Ani played. The notes echoed around him, filling the air with harmony. He realized he was staring at her, slack jawed.

As if she sensed his stare, she looked up and their eyes locked for the briefest moment. Or maybe he'd just imagined it. He forced his attention back to the audience.

Ani had more in her repertoire than just the piano concertos. Throughout the night, she sprinkled her performance with bouncier, more pop-like pieces. A trio of talented background singers accompanied her for those.

The audience loved every moment. He'd never doubted Ani's talent, but he hadn't expected to be completely blown away. Aside from her musical talents, she had an innate ability to connect with her audience, a star quality he wouldn't be able to put into words. Adam didn't know much about creatives, but he knew the combination of appeal and talent that Ani had was a rare gift.

By the time Ani stood up and took her final bow, several audience members were in near tears. He could hardly blame them. Ani announced the orchestra and her singers and took one final bow as the curtains closed. April immediately strode toward her from backstage but Ani was already making her way toward where Adam stood.

She gave him a brilliant smile that had his mouth going dry.

Without so much as a thought, he waved April off. He would take it from here.

"That was something, kitten."

Ani had to resist the urge to throw herself into Adam's arms. She knew she wasn't thinking straight. But some kind of euphoria had come over her sometime during the night. While she'd played, she'd almost had what could be described as an out-of-body experience. It was as if the audience had become an extension of her very being. Now that the show was over, she felt an exhilaration like she'd never experienced before. The looks she'd caught from Adam throughout the night only amplified the endorphins coursing through her body.

She'd done well. The audience seemed impressed. As did Adam. Hard to tell which pleased her more, as silly as that sounded.

"Thank you," she replied. "I had some churning in my midsection throughout most of it, I have to admit."

She wouldn't tell him the rest. She wouldn't divulge the crutch she'd used as she'd played. Thoughts of the time they'd shared aboard the cruise boat had settled her nerves and boosted her confidence as she'd been up there on that stage.

He'd described her as *attractive in all manner of ways*. She'd replayed those words in her head over and over as she'd played and they'd served to calm her anxiety. Maybe someday she'd let him know the large part he'd played in her successful performance. Right now, it felt too raw to try to explain it. She wasn't sure she could if she tried.

"Butterflies?" Adam asked.

"More like pterodactyls."

He reached a hand toward her before he suddenly dropped it to his side. Had he been about to touch her? "You hid it well," he said. "It looked like you were enjoying yourself out there."

She had to laugh at that; she'd been utterly terrified throughout most of the night. "I was and I wasn't. Let's just say I'm enjoying it now that it's over."

"That's to be expected for the first time. I'm sure the next one will be second nature."

"I'm not so sure about that." Her muscles were still quaking, her stomach still doing somersaults.

"What do you say we get you out of here? So that you can start celebrating," he suggested.

He didn't wait for an answer but clicked on his earpiece to confirm the limo was ready to take them back to the hotel. Then he led her to her dressing room to wrap things up.

She'd done it! She'd gotten through her first real theater performance as a solo act. And it could only be described as a success, Ani thought as she gathered her things. She changed into comfortable capris and a spaghetti strap tank, then slipped on a comfortable pair of flats. She'd deal with the removal of her makeup once she got to the hotel. And then she could finally relax. Maybe Adam might even join her and the rest of her team in some celebratory champagne.

All that mattered was that she'd finally be able to relax and wait for the grip of stage fright to slowly ebb.

Her phone pinged an alert for a text message. The tone told her it was Moira. Ani had half a mind to ignore it. She was more than ready to get back to the hotel and celebrate her little victory.

But knowing her manager, the woman wouldn't be ignored for long. Ani glanced at her screen.

Some early reviews are in already. Emailed them to you. You have to see for yourself!

Ani called up her inbox. And froze where she stood. An icy chill traveled down her spine.

The last email in her queue wasn't from Moira at all. It was another one from her self-described admirer.

You played like an angel tonight. Someday you'll be playing just for me.

She just wanted to get out of here, to have this night be over.

But the crowd had other plans when Ani and Adam made it outside.

His security team cleared a path for them, but Ani was tussled about and shoved nonetheless. Shouts for autographs, photos and the flash of cameras bombarded her as they slowly made their way to the car. Adam tugged her gently along while she struggled to fake a smile for the crowd.

"We're almost there," Adam reassured. "You okay?" Ani couldn't even be sure how she heard him through the boisterous noise.

"It's a little overwhelming." That was a lie. She was beyond overwhelmed. Even as she scratched out an autograph here and there, inside she was a turbulent ocean during a storm. Her performance anxiety was nothing compared to this.

And what about her stalker? What if they were right here? What if he was someone in the crowd, one of the people fervently trying to reach her? Ani knew it was highly unlikely, but the mere thought of the possibility had her stomach churning.

What seemed like an eternity later, Adam assisted her into the limousine and crawled in beside her. Her stomach clenched with residual anxiety.

Adam took her hand as he signaled for the driver to move. "Hey, you're shaking."

"I just—I guess I wasn't expecting that."

"We'll be back at the hotel in no time. Try not to think about the latest email for now." She'd told Adam about her admirer's last message right away.

Adam continued, "My IT guy back in the States is on it as we speak." He shrugged out of his jacket and draped it over her shoulders. "Here, I know you're not shaking because you're cold. But some warmth will help."

Ani held the tuxedo jacket tight against her. It did help. But his warmth through the fabric was the least of it. The scent of him surrounded her, the effect like a soothing balm on her frazzled nerves.

She uttered a small prayer of thanks that he was the one here with her. As nice as April was,

Adam's presence was much more comforting. She should have been better prepared for the paparazzi and the mob of fans. Moira had tried to warn her. But Ani was just so new to all this, focused solely on nailing her performance.

That email had arrived at the worst possible moment—just before she'd had to face a boisterous, reaching mob.

Considering that just a couple weeks ago, Adam wasn't supposed to have even been there tonight, it made for a curious state of affairs. To think, she'd fought her brother and father about having him accompany her on this trip. Now, she couldn't imagine what she would have done without him by her side.

Adam's phone pinged with a text message. He bit out a curse once he'd read it.

"What's the matter?"

"We might have a replay of what happened outside the theater."

"What? Why?"

"April and the others made it back to the hotel already. I'm afraid there's another crowd there waiting for you."

Oh, no. Ani felt the blood rush out of her face

and extremities. Her stomach clenched with apprehension. "But why?"

He shrugged. "You put on quite a show. You're probably all over the internet. Music fans everywhere are probably searching who you are and how you came to be here."

Ani rubbed her forehead, her hand shaking.

"Someone must have sent out some kind of social-media alert after your concert."

"I don't think I can face that again," she admitted. "Not so soon."

He squeezed her hand in his large palm and she could have sworn a palpable wave of strength flowed through the contact. When had she gotten so reliant on him?

"In that case, you won't have to. I'll take care of it."

"What? How?"

He tapped a playful finger on her nose and smiled. "We'll just have to take a detour. I know just the place."

Ani was shivering so much in the seat next to him despite the warm car, Adam knew he couldn't take her back to the hotel where a mob of people were waiting for her. She looked downright terrified. Which left him with really one other choice this time of night. He quickly fired off a text to a familiar number.

A response came back almost immediately with an added side note that made Adam laugh out loud. Ani sent him a questioning look.

He leaned over the divider to give the driver a new address, then sent another text alerting his team.

Ani still sat next to him, a virtual bundle of nerves. She was wound up like a tight coil about to snap.

"Try to relax. You won't have to deal with any more crowds tonight."

He could tell she had a lot of pent-up energy that needed to be expunged somehow. He was familiar with the feeling. A sudden burst of adrenaline in response to an unexpected situation always lingered long after the moment had passed. Adam had experienced it often enough as a soldier and many times since.

"Where are we going if not the hotel?" she asked, her voice trembling ever so slightly. Oh, yeah, she really needed some kind of release.

"Somewhere you'll be able to unwind a bit," he told her. "Looks like you could use it."

"I do feel a bit...out of sorts."

"It's understandable. Between your perfor-mance and the effect of the waiting crowd, I'm guessing you're still pumped up. We'll make sure to take care of that."

Her eyes clouded over with some kind of emotion he didn't want to speculate on. "What exactly did you have in mind?"

Damn him if he was reading anything too loaded into that question. Absolutely danger-ous territory his mind was trying to breach. Ig-noring her question, he leaned over and pulled out a frosty bottle of sparkling mineral water from the built-in fridge. "Here, we don't want you dehydrated."

She took it with a grateful smile. "Thanks. It appears you know what I need better than I do."

How could he answer that? He couldn't ex-actly tell her he felt more in tune with her than anyone else he'd ever worked for. Not even Tonya.

Don't go there.

Adam squashed the useless, painful mem-ories and focused on the matter at hand. Ani could use getting away for an hour or two. He suspected a mundane, normal activity might help her settle her emotions.

One thing was certain: he wasn't going to let anyone get near her as long as he was around.

"So, you never told me where we're going," Ani reminded him after taking a long sip of the mineral water.

"See for yourself," he answered as the car came to a stop. "We're here." He opened her door and helped her out of the car.

Ani looked up in surprise and took in their surroundings. "Where is this place?"

They'd arrived in Le Marais, a favorite spot of his. "Let's just say this a part of Paris that's a bit off the beaten path. Trendier and younger, so to speak."

The mouthwatering smell of street vendor carts drifted in the air. Adam couldn't tell which of their stomachs was the one that grumbled. "You hungry?"

She ran her tongue around her upper lip and he lost his bearings for a moment. "I could eat, now that you mention it."

"Good. You'll need something in your stomach if we're going to celebrate your performance with champagne later."

He walked her over to a crepe cart where a tattooed young lady with a silver nose ring was waiting on a lone customer. When it was their turn, Adam chose the sausage filling and ordered a strawberry-and-cream filled one for Ani.

"You sent the limo driver away," Ani commented as they sat on the curb eating their snack. A steady flow of people walked by them. Despite the late hour, the shops and eateries around them were full of tourists and locals alike.

He nodded. "Figured it would look conspicuous in this part of town." Plus, he didn't want the poor man to have to wait around until he and Ani were done.

She took another bite and seemed to savor the taste. "Mmm, this is so good."

"Let me taste," he asked without thinking. "It's been a while since I've had a sweet one."

Ani didn't hesitate before offering him her treat. Somehow, they'd reached a level of comfort between them that he hadn't exactly seen coming. It was easy to be around her, easy to talk to her. He could count on one hand all the people he could say that about.

Still, some things were better left unsaid.

Ani seemed to be studying their surroundings. Her gaze landed on a street musician and stayed there for several beats as she ate. "This is quite the place," she said between bites.

She was right. Le Marais had grown trendier and more popular year after year. It held all the charm of Paris with less of the staunchness of some of the more historic parts. His friend had done well to set up his business in this part of town.

He waited for her to pop the last piece into her mouth before standing. He reached a hand down to help her up. "Let's go."

"Where to now? We aren't leaving, I hope? I kind of like it here."

He shook his head, pleased beyond all sense that she was enjoying herself. "No. We just got here. Let's just say the fun hasn't even started yet, kitten."

Her eyes lit up. "Is that so?" She took his hand and hopped up.

"I just have one question."

"What's that?"

"Do you trust me?"

* * *

Ani realized with a jolt the truth of the answer that immediately popped into her head. She did trust him. Implicitly. Without even realizing it, she'd gone from resenting the way he'd been thrust into her life to actually needing him in it. If she examined the reality of her feelings even for a moment, she couldn't imagine being in Paris without Adam Steele by her side.

So she stepped off the curb and followed him without question, trying in vain to ignore the tingling along her skin where his palm met hers.

They soon approached the glass front of what appeared to be some kind of pub. It looked crowded inside and for a moment she hesitated at the door. Crowds didn't really hold a big appeal for her at the moment.

Adam sensed her resistance. "It's okay. You trust me, remember?"

With that, he pushed the door open and tugged her in behind him. Ani released a sigh of relief when a cursory glance confirmed that no one was really paying the newcomers at the door any attention.

A burly, thick-armed man serving drinks

stopped in his tracks when he spotted Adam. A wide grin appeared on the other man's face and he reached them in a few long strides.

Adam greeted him in French and the two embraced each other. Adam switched to English to introduce her. "Ani, this is Remy. We served together in the Middle East. He owns this fine establishment."

Remy offered her a dazzling smile and leaned to give her a polite peck on the cheek. He smelled of whiskey and fried food.

"Very nice to meet you."

Adam cleared his throat. "I mentioned we were looking for some privacy this evening. To celebrate a special occasion."

Ani gasped and braced herself for Remy to make the assumption Adam's statement must have invoked. It sounded as if they were looking for a quick tryst. She felt her cheeks flame with embarrassment.

But Remy simply gave a brisk nod. "Ah, yes." He pointed up. "The private party room is empty. It's all yours."

"*Merci*, Remy."

The other man smiled, revealing sparkling white teeth and a ridiculously charming smile.

"Of course, my friend. I only ask that you see me later so that we may catch up."

They embraced again before Adam led her up a side stairway. The party room Remy referred to consisted of several round tables, another well-stocked bar and a wide-screen TV mounted on the wall. A standard-size billiard table stood at the end of the room.

Adam turned to her. "How's your pool game, kitten?" Without waiting for an answer, he took her by the elbow and led her to the rack of cue sticks.

"Well, this ought to be interesting," Ani declared, choosing one of the shorter sticks.

"Don't tell me you've never played before."

She shook her head. "That's not what I meant." After all, there'd been a table in their family playroom for as long as she could remember. In fact, this was the perfect activity to take her mind off the stress and sheer rush of the past few hours.

Lifting a cube of chalk, she expertly coated the tip of her cue. "I meant it will be interesting to see how well you take it when I defeat you!"

Adam threw his head back and barked out a

laugh. "You're on. Ladies first. Go ahead and break."

She leaned over and did so expertly. The balls rolled out across the surface of the table and a solid rolled into the side pocket.

Adam lifted an eyebrow. "I'm impressed."

She sank one more solid, then stood off to the side while he took his turn.

A few minutes later, they were neck and neck, the number of solid balls to stripes at a dead even number.

Ani watched as he geared up for his next shot. This was a different side of Adam. He studied the table with an easy focus. She was used to him being fully alert, constantly surveying his surroundings.

She'd caught a glimpse of it last night during their Seine cruise when he'd let his guard down for a couple of hours. He'd been conversational and forthcoming.

But most of today, up until her performance, he'd pretty much been out of sight.

And now, he was treating her to a light-hearted game of pool because she'd been so frazzled after performing, receiving that unsettling email, then confronting an unruly crowd.

Would she ever be able to figure him out? The man was a complete enigma.

She scored a break in the game when Adam missed yet another shot. Ani saw a clear chance of winning. All she needed to do was hit the orange ball on the far side hard enough that it rolled into the green and sank them both.

She angled her cue and thrust it with a hard push and no small amount of force. Inadvertently, in her desire for a strong push, she somehow managed to slam her right hand into the left where it held the cue stick.

A stinging, sharp pain shot up through her wrist and up her arm. "Ouch!" The cue fell out of her hands.

Adam was beside her in an instant. "What happened? Damn it, Ani. If you've hurt your hand—"

She couldn't bear to think about it. The notion that she might have hurt her hand in the midst of a performance tour was beyond what her mind could absorb right now.

"I'll go find you some ice."

Adam ran behind the bar counter and came back with a plastic baggie filled with crushed ice. He placed it gently on the whole of her hand. "I'm so sorry, sweetheart."

"It's my fault. I was being way too competitive. Brant says it's one of my most annoying traits."

Adam shook his head. They stood inches apart. She could smell that alluring, woodsy scent of his that was now so familiar to her. He'd unbuttoned his white silk dress shirt just enough to reveal the tanned V of his upper chest.

And wasn't this one heck of a time to be noticing such things?

"No. I should have thought this through better. Bringing a pianist on tour to play pool..." He cursed again.

"Please don't blame yourself. You know how many times I've played this game without managing to hurt myself?"

"Do you think you've injured it?" he asked, his voice near desperate.

Ani took a deep breath to brace herself before attempting to wiggle her fingers. To her profound relief, the pain seemed to have subsided.

She released a deep sigh. "I think it's okay."

Adam's shoulders slumped with released

tension. He rested his forehead against hers. "Thank heavens, kitten. I would have never forgiven myself."

Ani knew she should step back. But all she could think about was how good it felt to have his skin against hers, the warmth of his touch where he held her hand juxtaposed against the stinging cold of the ice. Without giving herself a chance to think, she tilted her chin, angling her mouth so that it was a mere breath away from his. Her heart pounded against her chest so hard she thought she might faint.

Adam sucked in a breath. "Kitten?"

The breathless way he said her nickname sent a thrill down her spine. He was the only one in the world who called her that.

She found herself uttering the thought that had been on her mind since this morning when April had arrived with the bag of pastries. "You were gone most of the day."

I missed you, her mind silently added.

"I had to stay away." His answer was pained, his voice tight.

"Why?"

"Because of what's happening right now."

Electricity hummed over her skin at his admission. He'd purposely been trying to stay away from her. Did that mean he'd been thinking about her all day, the same way she'd been unable to get him out of her mind? The thought was exhilarating.

"I'm not afraid of what's happening now," she whispered boldly, almost against his mouth.

"You really should be, kitten."

A chill started at the base of her neck and traveled down her spine. She inched ever so slightly closer in spite of his words of warning.

Adam stayed stone still where he stood, the only movement the rise and fall of his chest with each breath he took. Ani knew he was ensuring that she be the one to make the next move. Heaven help her, she knew without a doubt right here and now the truth that her heart had decided long ago, perhaps even back as far as when they were kids.

She wrapped her arms around his neck and touched her lips to his.

CHAPTER FIVE

ADAM WAS HALF-AFRAID she'd step away. More afraid that she wouldn't.

How had they ended up here? Upstairs at his friend's bar in Paris, Ani Terrance was in his arms. And she was kissing him.

He knew he had to take it slow. Everything about Ani screamed inexperienced innocent. But heaven help him, he wasn't made of stone.

When he couldn't stand it any longer, he wound his arms around her waist, pulled her close against him and deepened the kiss. She tasted like home and redemption. Like the sweetest honey. He'd never get enough of her. She felt natural in his arms, like she belonged there, as if she always had.

Her chest rubbed against his and he thought his knees might buckle. She was so soft, her rounded curves enticing him like he was a man starved.

He had to ask her, had to make certain.

"Are you sure about this, kitten? Just say the word, and I'll stop." *Somehow.*

Her response was a low moan before she breathlessly told him, "Yes."

Adam didn't allow himself a chance to think. Cupping her bottom, he hoisted her onto the pool table. Her cry was one of pure sensuality and it drove him to near madness. He kissed her even deeper, fully exploring her mouth.

He stepped between her legs, pulled her even tighter, his palms spread against the small of her back. Then she wrapped her legs around him and he was certain he actually would go insane. She was putting him through the sweetest torture, making him burn with desire. She sighed his name against his lips and it was nearly his undoing.

Anyone could walk up the stairs at any moment and see them this way. Remy might very well decide to check on them. But Adam couldn't bring himself to care.

Nothing and no one else mattered now but the woman in his arms. He'd never wanted anyone so badly, so completely.

It was that very thought that served as a

proverbial bucket of ice water poured over his head.

What the hell was he thinking?

The stark reality was that he wasn't thinking at all. He had no business being here with Ani. He should have never brought her here, spent time with her alone. For all he knew, this was still the aftereffects of her performance high. She might not even be thinking clearly. The wisest thing to do after leaving the theater would have been to detour long enough to avoid the crowds back at the hotel.

Deep down he'd known that, even as he'd fired off that text to Remy. He'd brought her here anyway, ignoring the voices of reason in his head. To think he'd sworn that he'd learned from his mistakes.

Though it felt like losing a limb, he forced himself to pull out of the kiss and out of her arms.

The look of confusion combined with desire on her face nearly had him succumbing to his traitorous body once more.

He clenched his fists by his sides instead. He refused to make the same error in judgment that had led to such tragedy in his past. This time, he may not survive the pain and the guilt.

And Ani deserved so much better.

Ani blinked up in confusion when Adam stepped away. What had happened? Had she missed something? Perhaps he'd received an urgent alert on his phone and she hadn't heard it. But then she noticed the way he was avoiding her eyes. And she realized her mistake.

"We should probably call it a night." He gently took her by the elbow and helped her jump off the table.

"That's it? We're just going to head back to the hotel?"

He shrugged. "Your manager and the others are probably anxious to have you back. And I should go over some things with my team. We can talk about this…" he gestured with a wave "…on the ride back."

She had an idea how that conversation might go. And it mortified her. "Let me guess," she began, adjusting the straps of her bra and tank top. "You're going to say that we both got carried away and things should have never gone so far."

His silence was all the answer she needed.

"We can talk in the cab," he repeated, pulling out his phone.

"I say we don't even bother." She tried to brush past him to walk away but he grabbed her by the upper arm before she got far. For one insane and hopeful moment, she thought maybe he was again going to give in to the attraction so clearly between them.

He quickly nixed that notion.

"You have to understand I have a reputation to uphold. And there are other—"

She held up a hand. She really didn't need to hear any of this. The fact was he was rejecting her. After she'd practically thrown herself at him. "Honestly, Adam. I'd rather not get into a lengthy discussion."

He gave a quick shake of his head.

She continued, "I can guess what you're going to say. And you'd be right."

"I would?"

"Yes. I agree that we both got carried away by the moment. Being in Paris, a successful first performance, the champagne. You're obviously a very attractive man. It just led to a heady combination and I let myself give in to a whim." Her words were so lighthearted, she almost believed them herself.

"Is that so?"

"Absolutely," she lied.

So predictable. She was certainly consistent when it came to men. And how she would never understand them.

When they reached her hotel room, she was no less frustrated and confused. But she seemed to have put on a convincing act as far as Adam was concerned. He didn't so much as attempt to speak to her on the cab ride back. It looked like he had taken her words at face value. Somehow that made her feel less than triumphant. Rather, she felt hollow.

The feeling hadn't subsided at all seven hours later when she awoke in the predawn hours. Ani pushed her face into her pillow until it was almost too difficult to breathe. This was what happened when she let her guard down. She woke up alone and dejected the next morning, hating herself for falling so easily.

She bit back the sob that threatened to erupt

from deep within her chest. She wouldn't cry, damn it. She refused to.

So what if she'd thought this time things would be different. So what if she actually thought that maybe Adam himself might be different. He wasn't.

Peter had pushed and pushed for an intimacy she didn't feel for him. When she'd finally given in, it had been for all the wrong reasons. In an ironic and cruel twist of fate, now that she wanted that kind of intimacy with a man, it was completely out of her reach.

And there was no denying she wanted Adam more than she'd ever longed for anyone.

He clearly regretted kissing her. Well, regardless of what had happened afterward, she had no regrets herself. She'd wanted to kiss Adam, and she had. Damn the consequences. She'd nursed a wounded ego and a bruised heart before. She could do it again.

Snowball trotted out of his bed and jumped onto the mattress next to her. Ani gave the dog a snuggle. At least her pet was here to give her unconditional love. What more did a girl need?

Ani groaned out loud. She did need more in her life. Much more. But it appeared Adam

Steele wasn't going to be the one to give it to her.

Her phone pinged with the alert of a text message.

Are you up yet? We need to talk. ASAP

From Moira.

It appeared everyone just wanted to chat with her. Adam last night and now Moira. Ani would guess the latter wanted to talk about the former. Well, she didn't have it in her just yet. Not before a cup of coffee and a long hot shower.

She indulged in a hot, steamy bath instead and had barely stepped both feet out when a knock sounded on her door.

Adam?

Ani knew she was being all sorts of foolish. But the thought that he might be here to try to clear the air had her heart pounding with anticipation. He couldn't deny his attraction to her so easily in the light of day. For one, he wouldn't be able to use the champagne excuse. Or that she was tired and not thinking clearly so soon after playing for an audience.

Grabbing the thick terry-cloth robe hanging

on the doorway, she ran to the outer room to answer the knock.

The person standing on the other side of the door wasn't Adam. It was Moira.

Ani began to apologize. She'd completely forgotten about Moira's text. The only thoughts running through her mind during her luxurious soak had involved a tall, dark and handsome former soldier who insisted on driving her crazy.

Moira didn't look pleased in the least. She held up her tablet. "I'm guessing you haven't been online yet." She stepped into the room without giving Ani a chance to answer and shut the door behind her. "You should probably sit down."

Adam's early-morning run was cut short when he ran by a newspaper stand and caught sight of what looked like a very familiar image. At first, he continued running, convinced he was simply seeing things. But the image stayed with him and bothered him enough that he turned around after about half a block.

Damned if it hadn't been his imagination. Inserting euros into the slot of the kiosk, Adam lifted out a copy of the tabloid. He didn't even need to open it. He and Ani had made the front page.

They stood over the railing of a glass-covered yacht, smiling and gazing into each other's eyes. Their shoulders brushed against one another's.

Heaven help him, the look he was giving her was one of pure besottedness. Had he really been careless enough to wear such emotion on his face?

No wonder the photo editor had chosen this one for the cover.

Piano Star Spends Romantic Evening with Handsome Bodyguard Before She Dazzles Paris with Her Talent.

A quick read of the other captions only fueled his ire, as did the pictures and write-up inside. The woman who'd taken selfies with them aboard the cruise boat had apparently snapped one of the two of them alone when they hadn't been looking. She was quoted as saying that she'd thought Adam and Ani were "just the cutest couple" and had to snap a pic to show her American friends back home that Paris was indeed for lovers.

One of the inside articles was particularly troublesome. They'd interviewed another so-called security professional and had the man's exact quote.

One might wonder if a professional boundary has been crossed. He certainly seems to be guarding her closely.

Adam took a deep breath. He had to get a grip here.

With a baseball cap on backward and mirrored sports sunglasses, he didn't think he would be recognized. He had half a mind to keep going, just continue to run and complete the punishing bout of exercise he'd originally planned. Just pretend the paper in his hand didn't even exist. He certainly needed the exertion to help him vent.

But avoidance wasn't his style. He had some damage control to do.

Ani. What must she be thinking?

He had no one to blame but himself. He was the professional here. She was new to all of this. She was beautiful, talented and charismatic.

No wonder the world was already focusing so much attention on her. She'd only had one performance, for heaven's sake.

He had no idea how she might be handling this.

He pulled his phone out just as it started pinging with dozens of alerts and messages. So many people he owed an explanation. But right now, only one held his complete focus. He scrolled through until he found the messages from Ani.

Please call if you're awake.

And another one less than a minute later.

What do we do?

Followed immediately by:

How did this happen?

He typed out a response right away.

Sit tight. I'm on my way. Try not to worry.

His fingers started typing the word kitten before he caught himself.

He would figure out a way around all this.

Though how exactly he was going to do that was a mystery. His very reputation as a professional was on the line here.

Another thought occurred to him that had him swearing out loud—a passerby gave him a curious look and a wide berth. Brant and Mr. Terrance would no doubt get wind of all this if they hadn't seen it already. What exactly was he going to tell them?

First things first. He had to go make sure Ani was okay.

He called April as he jogged back to the hotel.

"Hey, boss."

"Hey."

"What's up?" April was the consummate professional. She would never bring up the gossip hanging over his head, would wait until he mentioned it first.

"Please move up your regularly scheduled morning meet-up with the VIP. I'd like you to go see her now. I'll join the meet in a few minutes. We need to go over some things."

He could have sworn he heard amusement in her voice when she answered, "I'd say we do."

Adam didn't bother to respond to that. Just waited for her to hang up.

He was a stone's throw from the hotel when his phone rang again. April was calling him back. That was not a good sign.

"Bad news, boss."

A brick lodged itself in the vicinity of his throat. He could guess what was coming.

"VIP not in quarters. Seems to have left the hotel."

Damn it, Ani.

He hadn't felt the need to place a guard at her door given the hotel's tight security and the manned elevator lobby on every floor. He would have to rethink that decision now.

"Did she inform anyone of her whereabouts?"

"Negative."

Adam pinched the bridge of his nose. Of all the foolish moves. He'd told her to sit tight!

A text came through on his cell just as soon as he'd hung up with April. A message from Ani.

Had to leave. Need air to clear my head.

He called her phone but it went straight to voice mail. He gripped the phone so tight, he thought it might snap in his hand.

He texted her.

Please tell me where you are.

Her response: I don't really know.

He closed his eyes briefly. Did you go left or right out of the hotel when you left? Which exit door did you use?

It seemed to take forever for the floating dots to appear on the screen. But her answer when it finally came through wasn't terribly helpful.

I just need a moment to myself. Please, Adam.

He had an insane urge to throw the phone clear across the street and into the Seine. Yep, he'd really made a royal mess of this one. He was personally involved in an international gossip story, his reputation as a world-renowned bodyguard service provider was sure to be damaged beyond repair, and the VIP in question was now in an unknown location.

Ani sat down on an empty bench overlooking the river and switched her phone off. She couldn't deal with talking to anyone right now. Even Moira had begun to test the limits of her patience.

Not to mention, she didn't want her phone tracked by her ever-resourceful bodyguard.

How had everything gone so horribly out of control? Here she was, trying to make a name for herself as a serious classical musician, and the only thing the world seemed to care about was her love life.

She snorted a humorless laugh. What a joke. She didn't have any kind of love life.

It vexed her that no one seemed to be talking or writing about her performance or her compositions. The primary subject seemed to be those pictures of her and Adam.

It was time to face an undeniable fact: she'd been woefully, naively unprepared for even the slightest hint of celebrity. It was a reality she had to examine closely and make some decisions about. A life of paparazzi ducking and tabloid features wasn't the future she'd planned on.

She reached for the paper-wrapped baguette she'd picked up along the way. The one Adam had had delivered to her the other day had been beyond delicious, melting in her mouth. But she found she didn't quite have an appetite this morning. She didn't bother to unwrap it.

What a sorry state of affairs. Here she was in Paris on a bright, sunny morning sitting on a park bench with freshly made bread. But she couldn't even enjoy it.

A shadow suddenly fell over where she sat. Ani didn't have to look up to guess who it was. "How did you find me?"

He came around the bench and sat down next to her. Even with everything else on her mind, it was hard not to admire the sheer magnetic appeal of the man. Dark stubble covered his square jaw. He was dressed in a tight navy blue T-shirt that accentuated his rock-hard abs. Abs she'd been running her hands over just last night. She had to suck in a breath.

"It's what I do. Part of the job is knowing how to track people down," he answered.

"Makes sense."

"You shouldn't have wandered off, Ani. You're in an unfamiliar city. And what the hell were you thinking, turning off your phone?"

"I made sure I wasn't followed. Well, except by you somehow. But you're exceptional."

"Is that some sort of rebuke?"

She merely shrugged.

Adam blew out a deep sigh. "Jeez, Ani. How

am I supposed to protect you if I don't know where you are?"

"I just had to get away, Adam. Surely, you can understand that." She took a deep breath. "April told me that last email was traced to the Dallas area. So I'm not in any danger from my so-called stalker."

"Still, what if you'd been recognized? Like last night?"

She grabbed the baguette and took an inelegant bite right off the end, just for something to do. Quite unladylike, as if that mattered at all right now.

"I'm wearing a wide-brimmed sun hat and large, dark sunglasses," she countered, still chewing yet hardly tasting the bite.

"Did it help?" he asked her. "Getting away on your own?"

"Not really. I'm still trying to figure out why anyone would find me worthy of tabloid fodder. It must have been a slow celebrity-news day."

He turned to her. Despite everything and all the chaos they found themselves in, Ani couldn't help but want him to hold her right now. She wanted to feel his arms around her. She wanted to go back to last night, when he'd lifted her up on that pool table. She'd thought about it all night during her sleepless tossing and turning. He'd crept into her dreams. Only in her mind, the evening had gone completely differently. Adam hadn't pulled out of their embrace abruptly. He hadn't walked away from her.

"You really don't see it, do you?" he asked, pulling her out of her musings. "The tabloids are interested in you because you're alluring and talented. People are drawn to you."

Was that really how he saw her?

Ani shook her head to clear it. She had to focus. They had more pressing matters at the moment. Her inconvenient attraction to this man had to take a spot on the back burner. For now. She wasn't naive enough to think she could ignore it for long. Sooner or later, she was going to have to grapple with her feelings for him.

"That isn't at all what I signed up for," she admitted. "Mysterious emails. Crowds waiting for me outside venues."

"Your life was bound to change, kitten. You had to know that."

She pulled the hat lower on her head, as if

she could hide herself from the reality of the world somehow. "I guess I didn't give it enough thought. I was too focused on the opportunity, the chance to share my music with as many people as possible."

"It will take some getting used to."

"If I decide to continue."

His head snapped up. "You can't mean you might want to give it up?"

She shrugged. She wasn't exactly sure what she meant; she just knew she had some thinking to do. "I guess I have some decisions to make."

"We'll figure out who's sending you those emails, Ani. It's just going to take some time. And you've worked so hard to get here."

He didn't need to tell her that. Hours of practices since she'd been a little girl. Sleepless nights spent composing after completing all her regular coursework. And now it was all being overshadowed by useless gossip.

"Maybe I'll just teach. It's not a bad way to make a living."

Adam reached for her hand, gave it a squeeze. It was hard not to think about where those hands had been last night: under her shirt, caressing her body… Heat crept along her skin at the memories.

Stop. Just stop.

"Don't come to any conclusions right now," he said. "You don't want to make any rash decisions."

Ani knew he was right. But the truth of the matter was that she was far more shaken about everything than she wanted to admit.

The only question was, what was she going to do about it?

Adam knew he had about a hundred other things he should be doing about now. There were several proverbial fires to put out. He had a team of professionals still waiting for an explanation and there were plenty of clients he should probably call.

So it made no sense that he was still sitting here on a bench with Ani almost an hour after finding her. As if they were a normal tourist couple sharing a baguette on a beautiful morning in France.

He felt Ani take a deep breath next to him. "Fame and publicity weren't supposed to be that large a part of this tour," she declared, staring off toward the water in the distance. "I haven't even been asked for an interview by a local television station."

"That was before you blew everyone away last night." *Including me*, he thought, though he figured that part was better left unsaid.

"Moira's trying to convince me to schedule a press junket either today or tomorrow before we leave. She thinks all this is a *hoot*, to use her word."

He broke off another piece of the bread Ani wordlessly offered him and popped it in his mouth. "I take it you're not a fan of that idea."

"Absolutely not."

"You'll have to let me know ASAP if you change your mind. That kind of event will take a lot of prep."

"I'm not going to change my mind."

"Fair enough."

She chuckled slightly. "Though the kids back at the center would get a kick out of seeing me online."

"You think about those kids a lot, don't you?"

A genuine, affectionate smile spread across her lips. "They're another reason I felt so rattled this morning with all that's happened."

"How so?"

The smile faded. "I can't bear the thought of walking through that center and having a random paparazzi potentially following me. I don't want strangers peering into my life. Digging into my past."

"Is your past so sordid?" he teased. He'd known Brant since they were both kids, and by extension knew she'd led a rather sheltered life.

She gave him a playful shove on the shoulder. "No. Of course not. But there's my mother."

Adam gave himself a mental thwack on the forehead. How could he have failed to consider how the loss of her mother would play into all of this?

"I don't want them so much as mentioning her name. Or how we lost her. My father won't be able to bear it."

A wave of guilt swelled through his core. He should have never let any of this happen, and he vowed he'd find a way to neutralize it somehow. How often in his lifetime could he let a woman down so completely when he was supposed to be protecting her?

"Maybe the interest will die down," he tried to reassure her. Though the comment was nothing more than a small fib. Each tour stop would bring more and more attention to her. She was a phenomenon in the making. He had no doubt of that after watching her from the stage last night and observing the audience reaction.

The real question was, was she ready for any of it? He had the feeling she was stronger than she gave herself credit for.

"Why do I get the feeling you're trying to tell me what I want to hear?" she asked.

"Is it working?"

"Maybe." She smiled at him, sending a silly jolt of pleasure through his chest. The smile slowly faded. "In the end, it's all about the music for me." Ani gave a weary sigh. "What no audience will understand is what the music means to me." Her eyes narrowed, staring off toward the distance before becoming unfocused.

"What's it mean, Ani?"

"It's a connection to my mom. Something we shared, just her and me. I think it's why I was able to handle her loss so much better than Dad or Brant. Why I didn't fall apart the way they did after she was gone."

It explained a lot as to why she was the one

left to gather the pieces of her family's broken hearts after the tragedy. "That was hardly fair," he told her. "You were just a child."

She shrugged. "Maybe. But I was lucky to have that piece of her. Every time I began to play, I felt her presence. My brother and father didn't have anything comparable. I was the lucky one."

She had no idea how selfless she was to see things that way. "You still had a right to grieve. In your own way." He was just beginning to understand how wholly she'd been denied that.

Her gaze found him again, her eyebrows drawn together, as if weighing the full impact of his words.

Adam's phone buzzed in his pocket before either could speak again, pulling them both back to the moment at hand. The damn thing had been going off continually since he'd sat down. He couldn't afford to avoid it much longer.

"You should really get that, you know," Ani prompted, then glanced at her own phone where it rested on her lap. "I'm ignoring mine but I'm guessing it's your team trying to get a hold of you."

Adam nodded. "Along with a slew of others."

"Others?"

"Current and potential clients. Not to mention curious friends and various acquaintances who suddenly seem to have found my number." Interestingly, he hadn't yet gotten any kind of message from Brant. He groaned internally. Not a conversation he was looking forward to.

Ani cupped a hand to her mouth. "Oh, Adam. I'm so sorry."

"What are you apologizing for?"

"For being so selfish. I hadn't even stopped to consider how all of this was affecting you."

Selfish was the last word he would use to describe her. Especially after the conversation they'd just had. He had wondered why she'd been so upset about the gossip sites and the tabloids. Her reaction had seemed disproportionate somehow. But she'd been worried about everyone but herself. Mainly her father and the kids she taught.

"Don't worry about me, Ani. You have enough on your mind."

"But what will you do?"

"Damage control. I can be pretty good at it." Except for that one fateful time when he hadn't been. He fought back the bile that threatened to rise up his throat as the memories assaulted him. The smoke, the screaming. The rancid smell of burned metal. And the utter, useless destruction.

Ani hesitated, then finally stood. "I'm guessing we should get back. Moira's probably ready to panic at my prolonged absence."

Adam nodded and stood as well. He watched as a small toddler ran after a ball toward the water with his frantic mother chasing him. She caught him just in time. The little boy giggled in his mom's arms as she carried him back to their picnic blanket.

Adam glanced toward the shine of the water, the rays of the sun lighting up the surface… then at a couple who held hands as they walked along and chatted animatedly.

Those were the images he needed to hold on to. The ones in his mind would only serve to drive him nearly mad if he let them.

"So, tell me about your team," Ani prompted as they leisurely walked back to the hotel. It was as if they were both trying to avoid the reality that waited for them.

"What would you like to know? I can tell you

I only hire the best. They're all former special ops or elite law-enforcement officers."

Ani chewed her lip. There were times like this when Adam was all business. "I don't mean their professional qualifications. Who are they? April mentioned she has a younger sister."

"Yeah, she talks about her all the time. April's putting her through college. Parents were deadbeats who wanted nothing to do with their girls once they hit the ripe old age of eighteen."

"That's very commendable of her."

"She's a woman of strong character."

They passed a charming patisserie, the rich scent of roasted coffee beans reaching her on an aromatic wave. It occurred to her she hadn't had so much as a hint of caffeine yet this morning. Just went to show how distracted she'd been. Any other day that would have been an unacceptable state of affairs.

Her gaze lingered on the doorway.

Adam must have noticed. "Would you like anything? Another baguette or a breakfast crepe, maybe?"

She shook her head. "I'm not hungry. But I could definitely use a cup of coffee."

He nodded. "Rich and creamy? Or bold and strong?"

"Something in between?"

He ordered for them both when they went into the shop. *Un café simple* for himself and *un café noisette* for her, which he told her was a strong espresso-type coffee with a heap of thick cream. The smiling barista handed them to-go cups in mere moments. They continued their walk.

"What about your other team members?" Ani asked, resuming their conversation. She was trying to keep her mind off everything she needed to think about eventually, all the things she had to figure out about who she was and the kind of life she wanted to ultimately lead. Plus, she was genuinely curious. So far, she'd really only gotten to know April, and not very well.

Not to mention, she needed to take her mind off of what Adam had said to her by the river. Had she really not been given a true chance to grieve her very own mother?

"Let's see," Adam began. "Tito is former navy. He and his wife welcomed twin girls about two years ago. That was when he decided he was ready for civilian life. So he started working for me. Believe it or not, the hours are better. And I'm a better employer than Uncle Sam in many regards."

She chuckled at that.

"Raj is going to school part-time. Mechanical engineering major through ROTC. He's looking to get his MBA. One of the smartest men I've ever met."

Ani took a sip of her drink as she listened. The savory chicory taste blended smoothly with the heavy cream. So much richer than the *café au lait* she'd been having. She would definitely need to order this again before they were due to leave Paris in a day.

Arriving back in Dallas was going to be a surreal experience. It was almost as if she'd be coming home a completely different person. She'd gone from being an unknown to having her image posted on numerous websites all over the world.

And then there was Adam. She couldn't define what was between them. But she knew for certain she wouldn't be able to stop thinking about him.

Adam continued, "Finally, there's Penelope. But we don't dare call her that. She hates it. Penny just got engaged to her high school sweetheart. She's excited to be moving into a new house once we get back to the States. I'm sure she'll invite you to the wedding. Apparently, it's going to be a huge one. You might not even be the only celebrity there."

The comment served as a reminder of all that she'd been trying to avoid thinking about.

Adam's phone hadn't stopped buzzing and ringing. The latest call had a shadow falling across his face when he looked at the screen. He bit out a sharp curse. The man could swear like…well, a soldier. "I have to take this."

She watched as he stepped away and spoke into the phone. His mouth grew tighter, a muscle in his jaw twitching each time he listened to whoever was on the other end.

When he clicked off the call and reached her side again, she could almost feel the tension radiating off of him. Tension and anger combined.

"Was it that bad?"

"You don't need to worry about it, Ani."

Again with the desire to spare her any upset. She reached for his forearm. "Please, just tell me. It might help to get some of it off your chest."

"I doubt it. But fine. If you really want to know, that was a client who just recently hired us. He wanted to know if he should maybe rethink the contract he signed with Steele Security. If he could trust me with his new young trophy wife to accompany her to visit her family in a particularly dangerous part of Mexico."

"Oh, no."

"The bastard didn't even want to listen when I told him I didn't even particularly do fieldwork. That I would only be leading the team."

"Adam, I'm so sorry. It was no doubt more his insecurity driving that phone call rather than any real concern about you." Not that the knowledge changed anything.

He drained his cup and tossed it in a nearby receptacle.

This was all her fault. He could very well lose business as a result of all this. Adam's reputation and that of his company would still be intact if her brother and father hadn't insisted on hiring him in the first place. The very livelihood of the employees Adam just spoke so fondly of might be in jeopardy as a result. She thought about everything he had just told her about the four who were with them today. And no doubt there were others he employed. What about all their dreams, their plans for the future?

She couldn't bear the thought that they may have to seek alternate employment because of an impulsive decision her family members had made. She hadn't really even needed a security detail. It was just another instance of the men in her life being unreasonable and overprotective.

An idea sneaked into her head. One that might take some of the attention off of the photos from last night. It just might work.

Adam would never go along with it. She had to be brave enough to do this without his knowledge or approval. He would refuse out of concern for her. She would just have to suffer his wrath afterward, if need be.

The local reporters wanted a press junket. That was out of the question. But maybe she would have Moira make a couple of phone calls to clear some things up.

Ani had no doubt Moira would love the script Ani wanted her to say. Her manager did love a good gossip story, after all.

CHAPTER SIX

WELL, IF THIS wasn't a first.

A woman was actually trying to spare his reputation. Adam would have laughed if the situation weren't so damn unfunny.

He rubbed at his forehead and reread the article on the website April had alerted him to a few minutes ago. He sat at the wicker table on the balcony of his hotel room. Though it was still early afternoon, he was having a sweaty bottle of American beer. Some days, a man needed a drink a bit early.

A spokesperson for Ms. Terrance finally returned our calls. She says the two have been friends since childhood and recently decided to take their relationship to the next level. Mr. Steele has been accompanying her on this trip more as a boyfriend than as her hired security. His profession just happens to be an added bonus.

It was actually quite genius. If he was here "more as a boyfriend"—quote, unquote—then he hadn't crossed any kind of line with a client. He took another swig of the ale. Ani's heart was in the right place. She'd done this for him.

Still, what the hell had she been thinking?

A knock sounded on his door, so light he'd barely heard it from his seat outside. He knew without a doubt that it was her. He could sense her presence almost before she'd even knocked. And silly as it was, he could swear he could smell her sweet floral scent in the air, even from way out here, despite the breeze.

He didn't bother verbally responding before opening the door.

She'd showered and changed since their walk earlier this morning. In a bright yellow summer dress with spaghetti-thin straps, she had a bright red scarf wrapped around her hair like a headband. The color combination should not have worked at all, especially with her bright red curls. But somehow on her, the look was delectable. In fact, she reminded him of a cupcake, good enough to eat.

Good Lord, snap out of it.

Ani rung her hands, hesitating at the doorway. "On a scale of one to ten, how cross are you?"

He didn't answer but instead turned around and walked back out to the balcony. Ani followed on his heels. He picked up the bottle of beer and took another swig.

"Adam?" She absentmindedly took the bottle out of his hand and drank a quarter of the remaining contents.

"Would you like one?" he asked when she thrust it back into his hand.

She glanced down at the bottle like she hadn't even realized it existed. She was definitely flustered. Well, maybe she should have thought about his possible reaction before she'd gone ahead and made such a decision on her own.

"Goodness, no. It's way too early to be drinking beer," she answered, without the least bit of awareness. "You didn't answer my question. Are you terribly angry?"

"You could have given me a heads-up."

"Would you have gone along with it?"

"Absolutely not."

She tilted her head to the side. "Not that I'm surprised, but why not?"

"There had to have been a better way."

"I couldn't come up with one. This makes sense."

"*You* didn't need to come up with anything. It was my dilemma to fix." He walked over to the railing and leaned with his arms braced against it.

"Well, something had to be done. Look at the client calls you were getting. And the publicity wasn't going to let up. You know that."

Of course, she was right. In fact, the next stop where she was performing could very well be worse.

It was just such a fiasco of a lie. "What about your emailing admirer?" he asked her.

"What about him?"

"News of you being involved with someone else is often the kind of development that would bring a stalker to escalate his efforts. You've gone and upped the ante."

She swallowed. "Maybe. Isn't it just as likely that he may get the hint and move on?"

She had him there. There was no way to be sure. No one case was like another. Infatuated celebrity stalkers didn't often have the same MO aside from the harassment itself. Ani was right. There was a chance her admirer would take this as a sign to move on to someone else.

Still, Adam didn't like the odds. "The point is, you shouldn't have made the decision on your own, Ani. Not without asking me. This isn't some kind of game. Your safety is at stake."

"So was your professional reputation."

She was altruistic to a fault. As if the two risks even compared with one another. Adam didn't know whether to thank her for her foolishness or grab her by the shoulders and try to shake some sense into her.

"It wasn't worth the risk to your personal safety."

"Very small risk."

"That's not your decision to make. Not in this case."

She studied him. "Why? On the surface, nothing's really changed. I still have an unknown person sending me messages, and I'm still under your protection. Why is it that you're so concerned exactly?"

She was much too observant and much too aware. "I'm your bodyguard."

"There's more to it, isn't there?"

Adam felt his fists tighten by his sides. "Let's

just say I'd like to avoid making the same damn mistake that cost me everything."

"What mistake?"

Adam braced his hands against the balcony railing. "Just drop it, Ani."

Ani straightened, then pressed her case. "Fine. Suit yourself if you don't want to tell me more. The fact remains that I did what I thought was best. Who knows, there might be paparazzi down there right now." She waved a hand at the street below. "Watching our every move."

Adam didn't think, just turned and stepped over to her, then pulled her up against him. Emotions he thought he'd buried suddenly surged to the surface.

Their lips were less than an inch apart. Ani's skin grew hot under his touch; her cheeks blushed a light pink.

"Then, seeing as the damage is already done, perhaps we should give them a show, kitten."

If this was supposed to be some kind of penance for what she'd done, Ani figured she was a glutton for punishment. This kiss was nothing like last night in the pub. Then, Adam had been gentle, his lips brushing softly against hers.

This kiss was the opposite of gentle. He crushed his mouth against hers, pulled her tight up against him.

"I don't know why I lose such control with you, kitten," he whispered against her lips. His words sent an electric current down her spine. He wanted her, he was admitting as much.

Right or wrong, she wanted him just as much, if not more.

"I can't seem to stop wanting to touch you," he whispered harshly. "We keep getting in trouble for it."

So he did indeed want her. He just didn't want to want her.

What a sorry state of affairs. Adam was probably cursing the day he'd taken on this assignment. It wasn't as if any of this was planned on her part. She hadn't walked into her father's office that day anticipating any kind of romantic junction in her life. In fact, she was at a point in life where any kind of relationship would be distracting and completely inconvenient.

She had thought she was on the cusp of the career she'd always wanted. Now, her whole idea of success had taken a completely different turn. Did she want the kind of success that came with fame and constant scrutiny?

She had way too much to figure out about herself before she could even consider tying herself to another person. Not to mention, Adam didn't exactly seem the type to settle down or be content with one woman. She'd heard more than a few times from Brant about his steady stream of romantic interests, always spoken with a sense of awe and respect. No, he was definitely more the type that left a trail of broken hearts in his wake. The last thing she needed was a broken heart.

She didn't come from the kind of folks who handled loss well. Or at all, really. Her father was a shell of the man he used to be, paranoid and anxiety-ridden.

So why was she still in Adam's embrace? Why was she kissing him and exploring his mouth with her tongue? Why was she moaning into his lips?

Her foolish heart leaped at what he'd said. He lost control around her. He wasn't ready for any of this either. But he was saying he couldn't help himself. His admission shouldn't have sent such a thrill of feminine pleasure down her spine.

If only she were the type of woman who could be comfortable with a fling. She could be up front with Adam once and for all. Tell him that they should just enjoy each other's company without thought of future ramifications. If only she could go ahead and indulge all the fantasies that had crept into her dreams since he'd come into her life.

The idea of it was oh so tempting.

But she wasn't built that way. She had to stop kissing him. Now.

Abruptly, but with deep reluctance, she made herself break the kiss and step away. Adam looked momentarily confused. He rubbed the back of his hand against his mouth. Then he gave his head a shake as if to clear it. "I'm glad one of us is using their good sense."

"It wasn't easy," she admitted.

"I should never have kissed you like that. I should never have risked where it could have led."

She could only nod. He was right. This was the first time they'd truly been alone together. The room on top of the bar last night had been secluded, but it had still been part of a public place. Anyone could have come up the stairs. Here and now, they could be assured of no interruptions. And heaven help her, if he'd led her there, she might very well have fallen into his bed.

He pulled his hair up off his forehead. "You should go."

"I know."

But it took several moments for her body to obey her brain. Finally, she turned and strode off the balcony and out of his room before she could change her mind.

Adam made sure to stand stone still until the door shut behind Ani. Only then did he release the breath he wasn't aware he'd been holding.

One time. It had taken exactly one time being alone with her for a few minutes in a hotel room and he'd lost all control. This was ridiculous. He was a trained military officer, for heaven's sake. He should be more disciplined when it came to his desires. No more.

And to ensure it, he decided to make the phone call he'd been dreading. Without giving himself a chance to hesitate, he pulled out his phone and dialed Brant's number.

He answered right away. "Adam, is everything all right? Ani?"

Adam was quick to reassure his friend. "Ani's fine. I just wanted to clear the air about something."

"What's that?"

"What you're seeing and hearing, about Ani and me."

"Yes?"

"I just want you to know it's not what it looks like."

To his surprise, Brant chuckled at the other end of the line. "Yeah, I figured it was some kind of publicity stunt. Knowing Moira and all."

"You did?"

"Hey, listen buddy, I'm heading into a rather urgent dinner meeting with some important clients. Can I call you back in a day or so?"

That was it? That was all Brant had to say about the prospect of Adam potentially hooking up with his younger sister?

"Uh…sure."

"Thanks, man." Brant paused. "Appreciate the

heads-up. But you know I trust you." With that, he disconnected.

Adam stared at his phone, somewhat stunned. He had braced himself for a much more uncomfortable conversation.

You know I trust you.

Adam threw the phone onto the mattress and swore. He had to wonder if Brant was a fool.

She desperately needed a good cuddle. There was only one male for the job. Ani curled up into the couch, holding her beloved mutt tight against her. For her reward, she got at least a few dozen wet tongue lashes to her face.

A knock sounded on the suite door and her heart pounded in her chest at the thought it might be Adam. But it was Moira who answered when she called out.

"Hey, I came by a few minutes ago, and you didn't answer your door," Moira announced as she walked past her into the room. "Where were you?"

Ani thought about telling her a small white lie. Moira's eyes seemed to light up with interest any time Ani mentioned Adam. She decided she didn't have the energy to vary from the truth. "I had to see Adam about something."

She was right. Moira wiggled her eyebrows suggestively. "Oh, did you, now?"

Ani released a sigh of frustration and plopped herself back down on the couch. "It's not anything to gush over. I just wanted to see if he'd heard about our leak to the press and how he was handling it."

Moira sat down next to her, knees tucked to her chest. "And how was he handling it?"

Memories of their kiss assaulted her and Ani felt her cheeks flame. "I'm not quite sure."

"Well. That's a good sign. Isn't it?"

Snowball jumped between them and nudged them both aside with his furry behind to make room.

"Again, same answer. I can't quite be sure."

Moira gave the dog a pat on the head. "Ani. What exactly is going on between you two? Every time he's by your side, I can practically see the sparks fly."

"There's nothing going on between us," Ani said, unable to look at her friend. Apparently she had the energy for a fib, after all. But at Moira's huff of disbelief, she had to relent.

"Well, there shouldn't be. The truth is, I can't seem to stop thinking about him. And I think he might be attracted to me, too."

There, now it was all out in the open. Not that it made her feel any better.

"Oh, there's no question about that. The man looks at you like he's starving and you're five-star French cuisine."

"Moira."

"No, seriously. He looks at you like he's dying of thirst and you're a fine Bordeaux. Like he's just wandered through a hot desert and you're a frozen vanilla custard." Moira giggled.

"I think I get the picture."

Moira's smile thinned as she turned serious. "So what are you going to do about it?"

"Nothing. Absolutely nothing."

"Huh." Moira tapped her chin, as if contemplating Ani's answer.

"After we leave Paris, I'm going to insist we switch to a different security service. If I even agree to more security, that is. This isn't an extended tour. I just need to get through one more performance and then I'll have a chance to reexamine some things as they pertain to my career."

"Oh, Ani, you can't mean that. You have so much talent. And the audience loved you last night. You were born to do this."

She wasn't so sure about that anymore. And the audience loving her apparently meant they felt entitled to intrude into her personal life. She'd never feel comfortable with that.

"I'm not sure I'm ready for all this, Moira. I need to think."

"You're scared, I get that."

She was right. Now that Moira had come out and said it, Ani had to acknowledge her fear. The whole world was watching her. What if she failed and made a fool of herself? And her growing feelings for Adam only served to complicate the entire matter.

She groaned out loud.

Moira gave her arm a squeeze. "I hate to add to your misery, but we have to talk about all the offers that have come in since you performed. Your limited tour could easily grow to an extended one if you're up for it."

Another groan escaped. She didn't think she was up for adding tour dates in the least. But she'd be giving up the opportunity of a lifetime. Her only mission before she'd gone up on that stage had been to prove to the world that she was good enough. Ironically, now that she'd done so, she was full of self-doubt.

What would her mother have thought? Mom was the one who'd set her down at the piano when she was barely old enough to walk. She'd been Ani's first instructor.

Some of her earliest memories involved sitting on her mother's lap at that piano bench. The instrument itself had seemed gigantic. Ani had found it hard to believe such delicate sounds could come from an object that huge. First Mom would play, and the music sounded magical and otherworldly to Ani's young ears. Then she'd let Ani run her fingers over the smooth, polished keys, encouraging her to press them down herself. She remembered cringing in shock at the sound at first. But Mom had simply laughed that pretty, melodic laugh of hers.

You'll get the hang of it soon enough, love.

Ani felt the sting of tears and pushed the memory away. Even the sweetest of memories could lead to crushing pain.

"Ani, I have to give these people an answer soon," Moira prompted.

Ani nodded and sighed. "I know, I just need to think about it. Just a few days." If only she could take off and go somewhere, to find some isolation and quiet and give herself a chance to breathe.

"Okay, sweetie. I'll hold off for now. And you still have that photo shoot tomorrow. There's no way out of that, it's in the contract."

Ani winced. She'd sort of forgotten about the scheduled photo shoot. Or rather, she hadn't allowed herself to really think about it.

"I know, I'll be ready. But can we talk about something else right now?" She desperately needed to quiet her mind. Why had she never taken up meditation? Or yoga?

"Sure. Anything for you."

Ani's relief was short-lived.

"So about this chemistry that you have with your bodyguard," Moira said. "Let's get back to that."

"Let's not."

"Why don't you just go for it? The man is hot with a capital *H*. If someone who looked like that was interested in me..." Moira smiled wickedly rather than finishing her sentence.

"I can't just 'go for it,'" Ani insisted.

"Why ever not?"

"Even you have to see that the timing is completely off. I'm not at a point in my life where I can handle the emotional pull of any kind of relationship. And he doesn't appear to be the type for heavy involvement, anyway."

"So why does it have to be heavy?" Moira nudged Ani's knee. "Come on. You're in one of the most romantic cities, maybe *the* most romantic, in fact. And there's a gorgeous specimen of a man who wants you. Just go for it."

Moira too closely echoed the thoughts that had been running through Ani's head when she'd been in Adam's arms earlier.

"I'm not one for flings," Ani said, despite the temptation thrumming through her. Except, she hadn't exactly had any deep, meaningful relationships either. Maybe it was just that she wasn't one for relationships in general.

"Wanna know what I think?" Moira asked.

Ani really didn't. Moot point, as Moira didn't wait for an answer.

"I think you're scared of more than just adding tour dates."

CHAPTER SEVEN

ANI WAS HIDING it well. But Adam could sense how nervous she was. The photographer's crew had cordoned off a good twenty-by-twenty square of the eastern side of the Louvre for her photo shoot. Tito, Raj, Penny and April stood guard around the perimeter. Adam was closer to where Ani stood posing.

Of course, they'd gathered a bit of a crowd. Ani had been doing fine until an audience had gradually shown up to watch. She kept glancing nervously at the spectators taking their own pictures.

Come on, kitten. Just a little longer. You're almost done.

"Let's take a little break," the photographer suggested.

Ani's breath of relief was audible from where Adam stood several feet away.

She accepted a bottle of water but made a

beeline right to where he was. A heady sense of prideful pleasure filled his chest.

"How am I doing?" she asked.

"You're stunning, Ani." She really was. They'd dressed her in a red satin formal gown, and her fiery red hair hung in loose curls over her elegant shoulders. "You'll have some great publicity images."

"I just want it to be over. I think I'm more nervous posing now than I was actually performing onstage."

She was clearly out of her element. He wasn't about to say it out loud, though. "Won't be much longer. Just listen to the photographer and focus on following his direction. This is almost like a performance, too."

She gave him a wide smile and leaned slightly into his shoulder. "Thanks. That was the perfect thing to say."

He put his arms around her, in a gesture of comfort, and felt her release a deep sigh against his chest.

The rapid-fire click of a camera sounded from where the photographer and Moira stood. Ani jumped back as if struck by an electrical shock. Moira gave them an innocent shrug. Ani rubbed her forehead wearily.

"It's okay. We're supposed to be dating, re-member?" Adam reminded her, though he felt less than comfortable himself. A bodyguard wasn't supposed to become part of the fore-ground.

"Perfect," the photographer called over to them in a thick French accent, "It's how you Americans say…worth a thousand words."

Adam's senses suddenly went on high alert. He took Ani by the arm just as a commotion broke out off to the side.

A man strode toward them with April fast on his heels.

Adam immediately pushed Ani behind him and widened his stance to cover her completely. He braced for a potential physical confronta-tion. But April apprehended the stranger just in time.

"I just wanted to ask for an autograph," the man protested in thickly accented English. "I was at her concert. Ms. Terrance, you were fab-ulous that night," he yelled, adding, "I'm a big fan."

Tito approached to take the intruder away.

"No autographs. And that's not the way to ask for one," he chided.

Adam allowed himself to relax. What the hell was April thinking, letting someone get past her like that?

She must have read his thoughts. April gave him an apologetic shrug. "Sorry, boss. It won't happen again. You have my word."

"What happened?" he demanded. Ani clung to his back and he reached behind him to give her a reassuring squeeze.

"I have no excuse," April admitted. "Just got distracted when the photographer started taking photos of the two of you together. I repeat, it won't happen again."

Adam gave her a sharp nod as his ire drained away. This was exactly what he meant about staying in the background. He and Ani had been the reason April had been taken off guard. He knew she was better trained than that. And she was right, she didn't have any kind of excuse. But he couldn't ignore the role he himself had played in the breach. This was his responsibility as well as hers. Just as much, if not more. After all, he was in charge. The last thing he needed to be was a distraction.

Right now, he only had one primary concern. He had to keep Ani safe.

He turned to check on her. Her eyes were wide with fear. Her entire body was shaking from head to toe; he could almost hear her teeth chattering.

"I th-thought you might have been right. That maybe the st-stalker had escalated his attempts, after all," she stuttered.

He took her in his arms, held her close. "You're okay, kitten. You're safe." Lifting her chin, he waited until she looked him in the eyes. She'd gone so pale. "We're done here," he barked.

His declaration was met with immediate protests from the photographer and his crew. Adam didn't care. "You have what you need."

Then he lifted Ani in his arms and carried her away.

"Here, drink." Adam handed Ani a stemless wineglass that she accepted with trembling hands.

She sat on his hotel balcony, the Eiffel Tower looming majestically in the distance, slightly covered in fog. "What is it?"

"Rosé with papaya juice. Just enough wine to take the edge off." He pointed to a half-empty, ice-cold water bottle sitting in front of her on the wicker table. "Straight water doesn't seem to be doing the trick," he added.

"I'm all right, really. In fact, I'm a little embarrassed. My reaction was disproportionate." Who knew she was so much like her brother and father, after all.

"You're still shaking."

"It's mostly residual. Subsiding as we speak." She held a hand up to show him.

"Still, you sure you don't want to see a doctor or something?"

"Heavens, no." At his look of concern, Ani felt warmth spread through her. "Really, I'm fine now. The rational part of my brain knows my emailer is nowhere near Paris. But my nerves are completely on edge."

"That's understandable. Who would blame you?"

"The autograph seeker just took me by surprise. I wasn't expecting anyone to get that close."

"He never should have," he bit out through

gritted teeth. "For what it's worth, April feels terrible."

She nodded. "I know. In addition to the in-person apology she gave me once we got back, she's been texting me incessantly to check how I'm doing and to say how sorry she is. Again." Her phone sounded an alert even as she spoke. Sure enough, it was April. How many different ways could the woman come up with to render an apology?

A sudden, disturbing thought occurred to her. "You're not going to reprimand her in any way, are you?" She would feel terrible if April got into any kind of trouble because of the way Ani had overreacted back at the Louvre.

"No. I have no intention of so much as chastising her. That would make me a hypocrite."

His words stunned her. "What are you talking about?"

He sat down across from her, pulling his chair so close their knees were touching. "April's not the only one who should apologize. I'm so sorry, Ani. I'm even more responsible for what happened than she is."

She reached for his hands where they were braced against his legs, and took them into her own. "The only person responsible is my so-called fan. And me. For the way I reacted."

"You have absolutely no fault in any of this. I was foolish. I repeated the mistake I vowed never to make again."

"What mistake?"

He gave a shake of his head. Whatever mistake he spoke of, it weighed heavily on his soul. "It's not important."

She wanted to argue. The anguish on his face told her exactly how false those words were. Maybe Adam was even denying that truth to himself.

Ani wanted to push for answers but it wasn't her place. She imagined he had seen and been through experiences she couldn't hope to comprehend. He'd been stationed in hellish regions and she knew human nature could be unbearably cruel.

No, she wouldn't push for anything Adam wasn't ready to give. He would share if or when he was ever ready. She could only hope she would be the one he'd turn to.

"Just know that you had absolutely no blame for what happened or for the way it affected you," he insisted.

Ani had to laugh, but there was no real humor behind it. "Well, I suppose we could go in circles all day abdicating each other of responsibility. I, for one, will try to learn from this. Starting with the lesson that I do not need to cower in paranoia every time I'm approached by someone who wants an autograph."

"That's hardly what you did."

"Pretty darn close, I'd say."

He rubbed the inside of her wrist. "Ani, you don't have to do that, you know."

She lifted an eyebrow. "Do what?"

"You don't have to pretend you're not struggling."

She released a deep breath. "You're right. I just wish there was someone I could lean on during all this. Someone like my mom."

She hadn't expected to make the admission. Had barely acknowledged it to herself. So it surprised her that she'd confided in Adam about it.

"I'd say you can talk to me, but I realize it's nowhere near the same as having a trusted parent to rely on."

Ani felt the telltale stinging behind her eyes again. Not a day went by that she didn't think about her mother or the devastation left behind at her loss. But since arriving in Europe, she'd felt an ache that only Mom would have been able to soothe. She swiped at her eyes before the tears could fall.

"I know I'm in a foreign city on the trip of a lifetime," she said, "but what I wouldn't give to be on a beach just soaking in the sun and trying to come to terms with all that's happening in my life right now."

"You have a few more days before you return to the States," Adam pointed out. "I could take you back early if you'd like to be back home."

She shook her head. "No, Dallas would be even more draining. Between my brother and father constantly hovering over me and everything I need to catch up on after being away."

"I see what you mean."

"I think I'll draw the blinds, sit in the dark on the bed and contemplate how I want to move forward in my life. Paris is a wonderful city, but it isn't exactly conducive to quiet pondering."

Adam looked off to the side, appearing to carefully weigh his next words. "I might have another idea."

"Oh, yeah? Consider me intrigued."

He swallowed. "It just so happens I own a place in this part of the world. It's not all that far by plane. Right on the Mediterranean. With a long stretch of sandy beach."

Ani felt her jaw drop. That scenario sounded like pure heaven. The man was full of surprises. "You do?"

He nodded. "Yeah. Ever been to Monaco?"

Adam could count on one hand all the impulsive, spur-of-the-moment decisions he'd made in his life. It was time to add another digit to the count. He hadn't realized he was going to offer to bring Ani here until the words had left his mouth.

He'd ignored the warning cry in his head, telling him all the reasons what he was doing was foolish. And all the ways he would eventually come to regret it.

But he'd seen the turmoil in Ani's eyes after the incident in the square, and all he'd wanted to do was whisk her away from it. Take her somewhere with no crowds to scare her. Somewhere only a trusted few people knew of. He'd only had one goal in mind—to make her feel safe.

For her part, Ani seemed equally surprised to have taken him up on the offer.

Now, as they drove up the winding cliffside to his villa in a convertible Mercedes, he couldn't bring himself to regret asking her.

"How often do you come out here?" Ani asked, shouting over the roaring wind.

"Not often enough."

Snowball let out a happy little yip in the back seat where he sat in a securely fastened doggy chair.

"But don't worry," he added. "You won't be walking into a dark, dusty, uninhabited house. I have someone I call in when I plan on coming into town. A local woman gets the place ready for me." Thank heavens for her, Adam thought. This time, he'd given poor Jaqueline less than one day's notice. Bless her to the skies, she'd agreed nonetheless. He would have to reward her flexibility handsomely.

"The thought hadn't even occurred to me," Ani shouted with a laugh. She already looked more relaxed and loose than he could recall seeing her since they'd left Dallas International.

It seemed a lifetime ago that they'd left the States. So much had happened since then. If someone had told him that afternoon that he'd be driving to his Monte Carlo estate with the VIP he was guarding, he would have laughed in their face.

But it was worth it just to see the utter relief Ani currently wore on her face.

He could relate. Despite the harrowing ride along jagged cliff edges, Adam always felt the tension slowly leave his muscles whenever he came to Monaco. The fresh sea air and the crystal blue water served as a balm to his soul. This was one of his favorite properties. He had to make more of an effort to get out here.

Though he hadn't seen this trip coming, Adam already felt good about the unexpected detour.

Minutes later, they were driving up the long pathway that led to his gated property. He fired off a text to Jaqueline and the gate slowly slid open. The older woman greeted them at the doorway.

"Mr. Steele. What a lovely surprise it was to hear you'd be coming." She was completely fluent in English, having been educated in Boston as a young woman. Not even a noticeable accent.

She came down the stairs and gave him a motherly peck on the cheek. When Ani approached with Snowball on a leash, the older woman clapped her hands with a grin. She leaned to pet the dog with a stream of French baby talk.

"Jaqueline loves animals," Adam told Ani above the fuss of petting and face licking.

"Snowball tends to make friends quickly."

When Jaqueline finally stood, he introduced the two women. The older woman's eyes lit up mischievously as she studied Ani. Uh-oh. He should have seen this coming. Jaqueline had been very vocal in the past about Adam finding a woman he could bring here more than once. She probably wasn't going to waste any time as soon as she got him alone to hammer him with questions. Also, she'd probably seen some of the online gossip. Jaqueline's hobby was social media.

Adam would have to worry about that later. Right now, he wanted to get them settled. He went back to the car and grabbed both their bags.

"I have a lovely dinner prepared for you when

you're both ready," Jaqueline announced, leading them inside.

"Thank you, Jaqueline," Adam replied. "We'll just freshen up and be right down."

He led Ani up the spiral staircase to the second floor. She paused to admire the view of the coastline outside the large panoramic window above the steps. Several luxury boats floated on the water, the sky was a spectacular shade of blue, and the water looked like turquoise jewelry.

"This is breathtaking, Adam. Exactly what I needed."

The statement and her genuine smile pleased him clear to his toes. Without thinking, he dropped their bags and reached out to trail a finger gently down her cheek.

"I hope it serves as the getaway you're looking for, kitten."

She sucked in her bottom lip, and he felt a wanton urge to leave the bags where they were and lift Ani in his arms and carry her like he had the other day in the square. Then he would carry her straight to his suite rather than showing her to the guest room.

Steady there. Ani was here for some much-needed peace and solitude. Not to be seduced.

He leaned down to pick up the bags once more as a disquieting thought occurred to him. "Just one thing."

"What's that?"

"I'm afraid I don't have a piano," he announced, wondering if he should have thought to tell her that. Or if he needed to invest in one as soon as possible.

Anything to keep that smile of contentment on Ani's face.

It hadn't even occurred to her to ask about a piano.

Ani had to take a moment to process that. When was the last time she'd gone so much as forty-eight hours without practicing her craft? What did it mean that the notion didn't scare her in the least? In fact, it felt oddly freeing. Foreign and unfamiliar, but freeing nonetheless.

What was happening to her?

It wasn't like her to accept impromptu invitations to grand estates. And it certainly was uncharacteristic of her to be so blasé about her practice schedule. But somehow, it all felt right. Being here with Adam felt right.

Ani plopped herself down on the king-size bed in the room Adam had led her to. Though "room" was an understatement. The closet alone was the size of her entire bedroom back home.

She'd known he was well-off. But this was a whole other level. Even after these past few days together, she knew so little of the man.

One thing was certain: it was beyond kind of him to bring her here. This would be the mini vacation she was due for, even if it was only for two days. Short but sweet. Hopefully by the end, she'd gain some clarity of mind.

A text message lit up her phone.

Heading down to dinner. No rush. Join me when you're ready.

Good saints above, she'd been so deep in her thoughts that she hadn't realized how much time had passed. Ani glanced in the mirror at the windblown disaster of her hair and her disheveled clothing.

This would not do. She'd unexpectedly found herself in one of the most glamorous parts of the world. And she would make herself presentable for dinner.

Adam would just have to wait. Her stomach growled in protest. So she'd have to get ready fairly quickly.

Another way she'd changed. Ani couldn't recall any time in the past when she would have let her hunger take a back priority to fixing herself up.

By the time she made it downstairs about fifteen minutes later, she had to think she'd made a pretty good effort. She wore a silk summer dress with a flower pattern and butter-soft sandals that she'd bought just for this trip. Her hair was mostly loose, with a small clip at the base of her neck securing it just enough to keep it off her face.

She walked through the foyer at the bottom of the stairs toward a door that led to a brick patio. Adam had given her a quick verbal layout of the house when he'd shown her to her room.

She found him there sitting at a set table studying a spreadsheet.

"Sorry to keep you waiting."

He looked her up and down. "I'd say it was quite worth the wait."

Ani hoped he didn't see the blush creep up her cheeks as he held out a chair. The night was comfortably warm with just enough of a breeze to feel refreshing. In the distance, the coastline looked like a masterpiece of a painting, majestic and artful.

"This is breathtakingly beautiful, Adam."

"It beats the army barracks."

She chuckled. "Tell me something. Did you happen to win the Texas state lottery at some point and neglect to mention it? I know a soldier's salary didn't allow you to acquire all this."

"You could say that. I've had a good deal of success with various investments. It's akin to winning the lottery. One particular tech start-up opportunity paid extraordinarily well. I invested the profits and the jackpot grew from there. Then I founded Steele Security and invested to make that grow."

He made the statement in a completely nonchalant manner, no hint of pride or boasting. She didn't know much about the stock market, but she knew enough to figure that this much financial success would require much more than luck. Adam clearly had a head for business and the intelligence to make extremely lucrative decisions.

Her curiosity was beyond piqued. "If you don't mind my asking, why are you still so involved with the company?" She motioned around her. "It appears you could sit on your laurels for a bit." He owned a villa on the French Riviera, for heaven's sake.

He shrugged. "I need to stay occupied. Not quite ready to sit on any laurels just yet."

Or he was still trying to prove himself. To whom, Ani could venture a guess. Adam had grown up with an aunt and uncle who'd been kind enough to take him in, but not enough to love him. They'd been ready to tell anyone who would listen that his arrival had put an inconvenient dent in their childless lives.

"You joined the army to get away, didn't you?" she dared to ask, knowing the question was more personal than anything they'd discussed so far.

"Ani, I had nowhere else to go. The day I turned eighteen, my uncle made sure to inform me that his responsibility to me was over."

Again, the statement was completely matter-of-fact, with no discernible emotion. "You don't sound bitter."

"They clothed me and they fed me for years. I had it better than a lot of other orphaned kids."

That was true. They just hadn't loved him. Ani itched to stand and walk over to pull him into her embrace. To try to soothe the unwanted teenage boy he must have been. All those years she'd been crushing on him as a teenager, she'd had no clue the depth of emptiness he must have been enduring.

Jaqueline appeared at that moment with a silver rolling cart. A bottle of red wine sat in the center.

"*Bonjour*, Miss Ani. I hope you're hungry."

Ani patted her midsection. "I'm starving. And that smells heavenly."

Jaqueline nodded. "Grilled fish caught just today. With a light green salad and freshly baked baguette. I've been baking bread all day."

Adam lifted the bottle and started to pour into their goblets. "Would you care for a glass?" he asked Jaqueline.

She waved away the offer. "*Non, merci*. I had a bit of rosé at lunch. No more for me today. Is there anything else I can get for you two?"

Adam leaned over to give her a small peck on the cheek. "You've done enough on such short notice," he told her. "Go on home. We'll take care of the dishes and the cleanup."

"*Au revoir*, then," Jaqueline gave him a grateful smile, waved goodbye to Ani, then turned to leave.

Leaving her alone with the man she was growing increasingly attracted to with each passing minute.

CHAPTER EIGHT

ADAM COULDN'T RECALL the last time he'd had such a pleasurable meal. In fact, he couldn't remember ever taking a full two hours to eat. Though the dinner itself had gone fairly quickly, they'd both simply sat and talked after finishing their food, slowly sipping on the rich merlot. He'd brought Ani here for her sake, but he had to wonder who was doing the other a favor.

"I think that might be the most tired I've ever seen Snowball," Ani said. Their conversation had veered toward the subject of her pet more than once. "He wasn't even interested in the bowl of food I set in his pen, just curled up on the pillow I threw in there and started to snore."

Adam chuckled. "We had a pretty long day of travel." It occurred to him he might be acting as a bad host. Just because he was enjoying himself didn't mean Ani wasn't tired and ready for bed.

"I apologize," he began, hating that he may be right and that Ani was ready to retire for the evening.

"For what?"

"You must be exhausted. I didn't mean to keep you up."

"You're not keeping me up." She took a sip of her wine, then glanced at him from under long, dark lashes. "Actually, I find I don't want this night to end."

Didn't she know what it did to him when she said such things? He was barely holding on to control as it was. They may be here in a paradise on earth, but the outside reality hadn't changed for either of them. He had no business wanting her, he couldn't offer her what a woman like Ani deserved. He had worldly possessions most men could only dream of. But Ani wasn't the type of woman who would make wealth any kind of consideration when deciding what she wanted from a relationship.

And he knew better than to pine for any kind of relationship himself.

He waited for her to continue, afraid of saying the wrong thing. Or saying exactly what he was feeling.

She finally spoke after sipping some more wine. "I owe Moira a call some time tomorrow. I promised to let her know if I'd come to any conclusions about adding performance dates."

Adam nearly laughed out loud. Talk about flattering himself. She didn't want the night to end because she dreaded the phone call she had to make in the morning. It had nothing to do with him. He shouldn't have been disappointed. In fact, he should have been relieved.

Focus.

"I still don't know what I'm going to tell her," she said, staring off into the distance. The sun was beginning to set, slowly turning the sky from aqua blue to a deep, dark navy.

"Ani, if you're not ready for a career move like that just yet, you have to respect that."

She toyed with the stem of her wineglass. "What if another opportunity like this doesn't come again?"

She really had no idea of the depth of her ability and talent. "You don't give yourself enough credit. I have no doubt the music world will be waiting for you with open arms whenever you're ready."

Ani finally glanced at him, and the turmoil

in her eyes had him aching to reach for her. "What if I'm never ready? What if I'm not cut out for the limelight and the life of a celebrity?"

"Then you should respect that, as well."

"Maybe. I'd have to live with the knowledge that I may have thrown away an opportunity most artists can only dream of."

He couldn't argue with that. *What if* questions always had a way of following one through life. But there was an opposite side to that particular coin. "If you go forward and you're miserable, you'll have the same questions."

She took a small sip of her wine. Adam got the impression she wasn't really tasting it, too deep in thought. There was something else weighing on her mind and impacting her decision about what path to take. The answer came when she spoke again. "I keep thinking about what Mom would think. Music was such a large part of her life. She was my first piano instructor. Some of my earliest memories involve stroking the keys while sitting on her lap."

Ah, so that was the missing piece. He should have known. Ani was afraid of disappointing a parent she'd lost long ago. It appeared they had much more in common than he'd ever known. But the difference was, Ani's mother was a loving and caring nurturer who doted on both her children. He'd heard enough about her from Brant to know that for a fact.

Adam had never experienced such affection. He really had no business trying to give her any advice about the matter, given his total lack of ability to relate. But he wanted desperately to ease some of Ani's turmoil.

"I wonder if I'd be disappointing her if I say no," she continued. "It's silly, I know. But I can't help but believe she'd want me to embrace this chance I've been given."

He reached across the table and took her hand in his. "Ani, I believe more than anything else that she'd want you to be happy."

"I should go check on Snowball," Ani proclaimed, then stood suddenly. She knew she was running from the conversation. But she wasn't ready to confront some of these feelings just yet. And she certainly wasn't used to sharing so much of herself with another person. In fact, it scared her how much she'd just shared with Adam.

She'd never told another soul, not even Brant or her father, the extent of her internal anxiety about letting her mother down when it came to her playing.

Adam slowly nodded. "All right. I'll be right here if you'd like to come back down."

Did she? Earlier she'd told him that she didn't want the night to end. The ocean air, the richly delicious wine and the magnetism of the man sitting across from her was a scene right out of a fairy tale that she wanted to continue forever. But then the conversation had veered in a direction she hadn't been prepared for.

"But I will understand if you don't," Adam added.

No pressure, and she was thankful for it. But part of her wished he would push her just a bit, take some of the decisions out of her hands.

He could ask her to stay with him. See where things might lead. But Adam was too much of a gentleman. That was a good thing, wasn't it?

She mumbled a thank-you before rushing upstairs.

As expected, Snowball was still out cold in the safety of his puppy pen. Too bad. She could have used an attentive ear right about now.

You just fled from the one person you've ever felt comfortable confiding in.

She had her reasons. She was just having trouble articulating what they were. Part of the issue was that Adam himself was so closed off, holding himself at a distance. Despite having known him most of her life, she didn't actually *know* him. Not even the most basic details of his background. Years ago, she'd asked Brant how Adam had come to live with his aunt and uncle, but her brother had shut her down, telling her it was none of her business and to stay out of his friend's business. Then he'd given her a serious noogie.

Ani dropped down on the bed and released a deep sigh. It bothered her more than she cared to admit that Adam wasn't ready to divulge anything real about himself to her. While she'd grown to trust him implicitly. The dichotomy made her feel lacking, inadequate. Shouldn't he trust her a little bit, too, at this point?

One thing was certain—she wasn't going to find out anything holed up in this room. Bouncing upright, she freshened up in the bathroom and went back downstairs.

Adam was in the kitchen, elbow deep in

suds, washing dishes. His back to her, he had his shirt sleeves rolled up and a kitchen towel draped over his left shoulder. Ani's heart did a flip in her chest. It had never occurred to her how sexy she would find a man in the middle of a household chore.

Not just any man. Adam Steele.

She figured she would probably find him sexy doing most anything.

She walked over and removed the towel from his shoulder. "I'll dry."

"How's the bunny rabbit?" he asked with a sideways glance as she lifted the first plate off the rack.

"Ha ha. My *dog* is resting comfortably, thank you very much."

"Glad to hear it."

"I suppose any dog you ever get would be much fiercer. The size of a small car, perhaps?"

"At least."

"I would expect nothing less."

Adam chuckled. "I worked with a canine unit for a while in the army. A German shepherd. He was trained to sniff out explosives."

Finally, a small tidbit of information about

his past. As innocuous as it was, it was *some-thing*. She'd take it.

"What happened to him?"

He shrugged, dipped another plate into the suds, then wiped it with a thick sponge. "Reassigned. He wasn't actually my dog."

"Do you miss him?"

He snorted. "About all I miss from those days." He dropped the last plate onto the rack a little too forcefully. "Brant was the one who gave you Snowball, wasn't he?"

"Yes, he rescued him from a local pound about three years ago when he was just a few weeks old. Just a tiny puppy."

"Brant was worried about you. Mentioned you were going through a tough time."

"I'd just been dumped. My on-and-off boyfriend of about a year decided our relationship needed to remain in the off status."

"What happened?"

She took the cutting knife he'd just cleaned, and dried it off with the towel before placing it on the counter. "The usual. He felt we'd grown apart. He said I never had any time for him, between my constant practice schedule and my volunteer work at the center."

"Brant told me he never liked him. He was obviously a blind and selfish fool."

Ani stilled in front of the counter. So she'd been a topic of discussion between Adam and Brant. The notion sent a hum over her skin. "Oh?"

"I asked about you from time to time."

"I see," she responded, taking a fork he'd just washed.

"You know, small talk during those long, boring patrols."

It appeared an opportunity had presented itself. Ani took the chance it offered. "You know, it just so happens I asked him about you as well."

Adam paused ever so slightly. "Is that so?"

"Yeah. Brant told me to mind my own business."

He reached into the sink to remove the plug and drain it. Several beats passed and he hadn't said anything in response to her comment. Ani concluded he wasn't going to when he turned to face her, leaning his hip against the counter.

"That's because Brant's a good friend. One who can be trusted to keep confidences that shouldn't be told."

She wasn't surprised by that answer, but she was sorely disappointed. She opened her mouth to speak but couldn't come up with anything to say. He tilted her chin with the tip of his finger.

"Good night, kitten. I'll see you in the morning."

Ani had Snowball out in the grassy area by Adam's infinity pool when she noticed him coming up the stone steps. Dressed in sports shorts and a T-shirt that accentuated all the contours of his muscles, and judging by the sheen of sweat over his tanned skin, he'd clearly been out for a run.

"You're up," he said when he spotted her. He reached down to give the dog an affectionate pat.

"I slept longer than I usually do," she answered. She wouldn't share that she'd only overslept because she'd had so much trouble drifting off once she got into bed. Her mind had been busy all night with thoughts of the man who stood before her. Snippets of their conversation over dinner, the way she'd felt in his arms when he'd carried her out of the square. The feel of his lips against hers when he'd kissed her on the hotel balcony. She'd tossed and turned until the light of dawn had crept through her window.

"Probably the fresh sea air."

"Right," she replied simply. "You've obviously been up for a while."

He wiped away the sweat on his chin with his forearm. "Went for a quick run along the beach. Go ahead and grab some breakfast. Jaqueline stopped by with some pastries earlier. Cheese-filled croissants."

"That sounds heavenly." But what she could really use was caffeine.

Adam must have read her thoughts. "And there's a carafe full of freshly brewed American coffee. I always keep some on hand."

"Perfect."

He gave her a wink and a smile that had her stomach doing a small dive. "I'll be back after a quick shower."

True to his word, Ani had barely had a chance to pour her coffee and grab a croissant when he ran back down to join her at an outdoor patio table. His hair was still dripping wet, and he'd barely bothered to comb it. The result was a

disheveled, tousled look that she found ridiculously sexy.

He was wearing swim trunks.

"Did you pack a suit?" he asked as he sat
with his own mug of coffee. "You did say you
wanted some time on a beach. If not, we can
pick one up from one of the boutiques."

"I have a suit. And spending time on the
beach sounds like exactly what the doctor ordered." Also, it would give her an excuse to
delay calling Moira.

"Eat your breakfast, then go throw your suit
on. I'll play fetch with your pet rabbit."

Ani bit back her laugh. "Please don't call him
that," she said with mock outrage. "He can hear
you."

Twenty minutes later, Adam proved true to
his word. Snowball was panting heavily and re-
fusing to retrieve a stick Adam had just thrown.

"Looks like this fella could use a midmorn-
ing nap," she said. "I'll take him up to my room
and get him settled."

He wiggled his eyebrows. "I'll be waiting."

Ani was on her way back downstairs when
the front door opened into the foyer. Jaqueline
stepped inside, carrying paper bags of various

sizes. The enticing aroma of fresh bread suddenly filled the air.

Ani strode over to her. "Here, let me help with some of those."

"Merci," the other woman replied, handing her some of the bags. "I thought I'd get started on lunch."

The French certainly knew how to eat, Ani mused. At this rate, she'd have to shop for new clothes upon her return to Dallas.

Jaqueline suddenly stopped and scrutinized her face. Had she left a smudge of sunscreen unblended? Ani rubbed at her cheek.

"Forgive me for staring, dear," Jaqueline said with a warm smile. "I'm just so glad Adam has brought someone here finally. Usually, when he visits, he takes a morning run and then holes up in his study for the rest of the day just working."

Ani wasn't sure what to say to that. In fact, the unexpected conversation was throwing her off balance.

Jaqueline continued, "I'm glad he's finally found someone to distract him from all that work he does."

It appeared she had come to all sorts of conclusions about the two of them.

Ani finally found her tongue. "Oh, it's not like that. I just had a tough couple of days and he brought me here to unwind. We're not, like, together in that way."

But what exactly were they? There was no denying the attraction between them. Nor the way he'd seemed just as affected by their kisses as she was.

Jaqueline ignored her. "You know, the last time he brought a woman here, it didn't go so well. She ended up leaving in a huff. You probably know of her. That model that does the perfume ads."

"Oh?" was all Ani could muster. Adam had dated a famous perfume model. She'd been here at this very villa with him. "Were they very serious?" She couldn't help but ask.

"I think so." Jaqueline awkwardly squeezed her arm in reassurance while still clutching a bag. "But don't worry, he seems to be having more fun with you. He's smiling more."

Ani felt her heart sink and she nearly dropped the parcel she was holding. Of course she'd known that Adam must have been involved romantically with other women. But hearing he might have been serious with someone triggered a tightening in the pit of her stomach. A well-known perfume model, no less.

"How long ago was this?" She had to ask, a glutton for punishment.

She didn't get an answer.

Instead, Adam loudly cleared his throat behind them.

When she turned and saw the expression on his face, Ani lost her grip on the bag. It landed on the floor with a thud.

CHAPTER NINE

THE WALK DOWN the rocky path toward the
beach was thick with tension. On the one hand,
Ani could see why Adam might be cross. She
had been caught gossiping about him with the
woman who served as his housekeeper. On the
other hand, what was the big deal? So much for
relaxing with some sun and sand by the water.

The sight that greeted her when they reached
the bottom nearly took her breath away. It was
the bluest water she'd ever seen. Majestic yachts
floated in the distance. The cliffside was dotted
with buildings and structures built right into
the mountain. She paused to admire the view.
Adam kept right on walking.

That was it. She'd had enough of the grumpy
silent treatment. Catching up, she grabbed his
elbow and made him turn around to face her.

"Is there a problem?" He wanted to know.

"You tell me."

"If you had a question, you should have asked me. Not Jaqueline."

It was hard to read his eyes behind the mirrored glasses. But his tone was all too clear.

"For the record," Ani said, "Jaqueline started the conversation. And yes, I should have come to you with any questions that arose from it. But I don't see why you're so irate about the whole thing."

"Don't you?"

"Let me ask you, would you have told me anything about your past if I'd asked you?"

"It depends on what you wanted to know."

Ani crossed her arms in front of her chest. "That's a tad hypocritical, don't you think?"

It was the wrong word. A muscle twitched along his jawline. He pulled his arm free. "Care to explain what you mean by that?"

She wasn't going to do this. There was absolutely no need for this conversation. She'd thought perhaps they were growing close. That maybe he was growing to care for her a bit. But she'd been wrong. Because here he was, nearly livid at the possibility that she might have learned a thing or two about him.

"Never mind," she bit out. "This is pointless."

After tomorrow, this whole sad state of affairs would be over and they could both go their separate ways. If she did decide on going on the additional tour dates, she would have to find another security service. She'd have to look for a bodyguard with a better disposition, for one.

She ran past him toward the water. Her skin was burning hot with irritation. Stripping off her summer dress, she made straight for the ocean and dove in when she'd gone far enough out. The saltwater felt cool and soothing. To her surprise, Adam was standing less than a foot in front of her when she resurfaced. Shirtless and wet from the chest down.

How had he gotten here so fast? She'd had a good twenty feet on him at one point. He'd even had time to rid himself of his shirt and sunglasses.

"You didn't answer my question," he pointed out.

Oh, yes. He was perturbed that she had called his actions hypocritical. It was her turn to get angry. Out of pure frustration, she hooked her leg around the back of his knee and pushed against his chest with all her might.

It must have been shock, because Adam went down with a resounding splash into the water.

She came this close to laughing. Until he shot up out of the water to glare at her. "Feel better?" he demanded.

"I could ask you the same question. Clearly, you needed to cool off a bit."

"Looks like someone schooled you in some self-defense moves." He wiped down his face with the palm of his hand.

"Just what the teenage boys at the center showed me."

"You learned well."

She sat back, allowing herself to float. "That makes me realize something I hadn't thought about before."

"What's that?"

"You've been derelict in your duty. Shouldn't you have been teaching me some self-defense moves yourself?"

He narrowed his eyes in question. "What?"

"Most movies and books involving bodyguards have at least one scene where the woman is soundly yet cautiously manhandled while the so-called protector shows her how to defend herself."

"Is that so?"

She nodded. "I shouldn't have to tell you this."

He gave her such a casual shrug her instincts went on high alert. "It's not too late. I could start right now."

She squinted at him, not liking the sound of his voice at all. "What did you have in mind?"

"Every time you manage to take me down again, you can ask me a question."

Ha! As if she trusted him to really reveal anything.

He continued as if he'd read her mind. "I promise to answer whatever the question is. Fully and truthfully."

She was intrigued despite herself. Darned if she'd show it, however. "Maybe I'm not that interested any longer," she threw out.

"Maybe you're a liar."

That did it. She did want to topple him over again. But she wouldn't have the advantage of surprise this time.

"I don't want to hurt you, Adam."

For the first time since he walked in on her and Jaqueline in the foyer, she saw the hint of a smile on his face. "Feel free to try, kitten."

"Fine." She stood up in the soft sand.

Trying the same maneuver again, she went to hook her foot behind his knee. He stepped away before she could so much as reach him.

He smirked at her.

Making the perfect fist, she got ready to aim for his side. Not really to hurt him, just to throw him off balance so she could trip him into the water. He grabbed her wrist before she could make contact.

A fake-out. It was her only hope. She threw her hands up in the air as if completely frustrated. Not that she wasn't. "Fine, you win. I'm going back onto the shore."

Pretending to stride by, she bent over and lunged her shoulder toward him instead. He barely moved.

"Oh, kitten. I was hoping you could do better than that."

"Yeah, well, so was I."

Was it her imagination, or was that actual amusement she saw in his eyes? At her expense!

He rubbed his chin. "Perhaps you're right. Maybe I should show you some basic jujitsu moves."

"Jaja what now?"

He actually laughed. "Here. I know you're dying to see me fall in again. A freebie." He reached for her stealthily, without warning. "But you're coming with me."

Before she knew what he intended, he launched himself backward into the water, pulling her on top of him.

What had he been thinking?

Ani landed on his chest, his arms around her midriff. He still held her as they broke the surface of the water a second later. And now he could hardly think at all. She'd thrown her arms around his neck at some point. Now they stood, their faces an inch apart, skin against wet skin.

"That was uncalled for." Her breath was thick when she spoke. "You owe me an apology."

He wasn't sure if they were speaking of the stunt he just pulled or what had happened between them back at the house. He decided he didn't care. It was hard to care about anything but the feel of her when she was in his arms like this. "I'm sorry," he whispered.

"Me, too," she said, surprising him. "I'm sorry, Adam."

"What exactly are *you* apologizing for, kitten?"

"For upsetting you earlier."

Adam swallowed. At the time, he'd been beyond annoyed. Now he felt like a heel for the way the scene had played out. He just wasn't used to talking about himself. He didn't want to think about his past, let alone have it be a topic of discussion.

"And I'm sorry for this," she said on a breathless whisper, just before touching her lips to his.

The blood pounded in his veins. Her hesitant, gentle kiss threw the last gates of his resolve wide open. He pulled her tighter against him, plunged deeper into her mouth. Her arms grew tighter around his neck. Hooking his hands at the backs of her thighs, he lifted her to wrap her legs around his waist.

Time seemed to stand still; he couldn't get enough of her. Every nerve ending in his body was burning with desire. He had no idea how long he stood there in the water, holding her and tasting her. Finally, a small cry of sanity cut though his desire-fogged brain. He somehow managed to break the kiss.

"We need to stop, kitten. Or I'm likely to carry you out behind one of the cliffs and..." He knew better than to put into words all the things he was thinking.

She blinked up at him. The heat in her eyes nearly had his knees buckling beneath him.

He doubted the depth of her desire could match his own. Reluctantly, he disentangled their bodies, though he felt the ache of the loss clear to his bones.

Ani gave her head a shake.

By the time they made it back to shore, Adam almost had his breathing back under control. Almost.

"Guess we should have thought to bring towels," she muttered as she pulled her dress over her wet body. The fabric clung to her curves and Adam nearly groaned out loud.

"I thought we'd walk along the sand for a while," he answered. "I wasn't really expecting to go for a swim quite so soon."

"Well, I wasn't expecting any of that." She plopped down on the ground, shifting her legs underneath her.

Adam dropped down next to her. "That makes

two of us. Though I guess I should have been better prepared."

"What's that mean?" Picking up a handful of sand, she let the grains slowly sift through her fingers.

"It means we're from two different worlds." He looked off toward the horizon. "You asked in Paris how I came to live with my aunt and uncle. Would you like to know the full story?"

"Of course. All I ever heard was just rumors that can't all be true because many of them contradicted each other. You were a bit of a novelty. Everyone talked about you."

He grunted a humorless laugh. "The reality wasn't novel at all. My old man took off and my mom chased after him. He left because he didn't want the burden of a family. And she chose him over me, her son. Last I heard, he sobered up and cleaned himself up. They have a whole other family. They still wanted nothing to do with me. Until learning about my wealth, that is… Now I hear from them all the time."

"I take it you ignore them."

He shrugged. "I ignore my parents, yes, but I have a younger brother and sister. They're actually pretty cute." Was that a hint of pride she heard in his voice? "I make sure they're taken care of."

"Taken care of how?"

"I send them a monthly stipend. I have a PI check in regularly to make sure the money is being spent where it should be and not on party expenses for two people who only ever thought of me as unwanted."

"Adam, I'm so sorry. I wish I'd known."

The pitying tone of her voice was exactly why she hadn't known all this time. Why he hadn't spoken of it with anyone but Brant, who'd been decent enough to keep it to himself all these years.

"Would it have made a difference if you had known?" he asked.

She looked at him then, her beautiful dark eyes wide with understanding. "It would have to me. All those times, I felt so out of place whenever you and Brant hung out together. So unwanted."

"I'm genuinely sorry about that. I was a thoughtless heel back then to make you feel that way."

He'd tried so hard to hide his feelings for her as a way to protect himself. She'd been so far out of his league. Just as she was now. He may be proficient in a few languages and enjoy a professional success few could dream of, but most of that had been pure luck. Ani had been born into a well-known and respected family and she was on her way to worldwide success. He simply didn't measure up.

He couldn't say any of that out loud. He'd tried so hard when they were kids to get Ani to believe he found her annoying, that he didn't want her around. The exact opposite had been true. And it had scared him to death.

Judging by the way he was feeling now, he'd been right to be scared.

Ani followed Adam as they walked back up the pathway that led to the house, both still dripping wet. She didn't know what to make of him. He seemed determined to push her away the moment they got too close.

"I think we should head to the casino this evening," Adam announced, pulling her out of her thoughts with a completely unexpected suggestion. "I'm sure Jaqueline would be happy to sit with Snowball. She seems to be quite fond of him. How's your blackjack game?"

"Nonexistent. I don't even know how to play."

"We'll have you rolling dice then, that's simple enough to learn."

If this was Adam's attempt to distract her from their earlier conversation, she wasn't sure it was going to work.

"I think we could both use a night out," he added. "What do you say?"

"I don't know if I have anything appropriate to wear. I didn't pack any of my formal attire that I brought along for the performances."

They'd reached the patio outside his villa. "There's a gown or two that should be hanging—" He caught himself just in time.

"I take it the perfume model left a few items behind in her hasty departure?"

To his credit, he looked properly chagrined.

Doubtful the woman's discards would fit Ani, anyway. She was probably tall and statuesque with ample curves in all the right places.

"I never got around to asking Jaqueline to clear them out. We can stop at one of the boutiques later today," Adam said. "Pick something up for you."

She shrugged. "I suppose that would work."

He paused, then took her by the hand. "Listen, Ani. The model wasn't anyone I was ever serious with."

"Oh?" She wasn't quite sure what else to say. He'd surprised her.

He nodded. "I was at a point in my life when I needed a distraction with no strings attached. She fit the bill."

"I see."

"I got the impression she needed a distraction as well. But I didn't bother to ask. And she didn't ask me either."

Ani could only remain silent as he went on. "We had some fun together while it lasted. But she's not someone I even often think of."

With that, he pulled away and turned to walk into the house. Leaving Ani with one question on her mind. Who was the woman from his past Adam *did* think about?

The first boutique they visited, Ani managed to find the perfect dress: a strapless velvet gown in a midnight burgundy. Now, back at Adam's estate, she studied the end result in the floor-length mirror of her closet. The color shouldn't have worked with her bright red hair but somehow it flattered her, if she did say so herself.

Adam hadn't seen it on her yet. She wondered if he would like it as well.

The man was a complete enigma. She knew he wanted her; the way he kissed her left no doubt. But he always held something back. And he'd blown her mind with all the things he'd revealed today. Still, she couldn't help but feel there was another piece of the puzzle missing when it came to understanding who he was behind the successful soldier turned billionaire business tycoon.

She turned to study her reflection from behind. She'd never been to any kind of casino before, let alone one known all over the world and featured in countless movies. But she figured she'd be passable.

It had taken her a while to warm to the idea, but she was growing more and more excited for the evening ahead with each passing minute. Tonight was going to be an opportunity to escape reality and ignore all the concerns that had been pulling at her these past few days. From anxiety about her career to the demands from Moira and others at the label, to the pressure of appeasing her family...and then there was Adam.

As far as he was concerned, she would just have to pretend. She'd let him take her by the elbow and walk her into an exclusive casino as if they were a real couple with a real future.

She much preferred that fictional scenario to the uncertainty she seemed to be facing in every aspect of her life.

CHAPTER TEN

SHE WAS LOSING a good amount of his money, Adam thought as he watched Ani throw another bad roll. Yet another stack of her chips was swept away by the dealer. It was worth it to see the genuine smile on her face. She was thoroughly enjoying herself. Considering the limited time they had before they each returned to reality, he was happy to see her letting loose a little. But her stack had most definitely dwindled in a shockingly short amount of time.

He would have to go get her more. After this next round, though, he was going to have to cut her off. She was just so bad at this and luck didn't seem to be on her side tonight. He happened to be a wealthy man but there were countless other entities he would rather donate his funds to rather than one of the richest casinos in the world.

Besides, she might have better luck at one of the slots. It certainly couldn't be worse.

He returned with another silver bucket full of chips only to find Ani had left the craps table. He spotted her over at the wide curved mahogany bar.

She was talking to a man. A handsome man in an expertly cut tuxedo.

Adam felt his fingers tighten around the rim of the bucket. Silly, really—he had no claim to her. She had every right to speak with any man in here. It made no sense that he wanted to body slam the man into the bar and wipe that charming smirk off his face.

He approached just as he heard Ani decline a drink offer. "Adam! There you are. This is Martin. He works for the Opéra de Monte-Carlo. It's part of the casino. Martin, this is my friend, Adam."

Adam knew he hadn't imagined the way Martin's smile had grown wider and Ani's use of the term *friend*.

The two men exchanged pleasantries in a mixture of both English and French. Adam held up the bucket full of chips toward Ani. "I got you more."

She tilted her head and smiled. "I decided to

quit. Turns out I'm not very good at the craps table."

"We'll have you try the slots then." He gently took her by the elbow and led her away.

Ani stumbled but ultimately followed him, offering an apologetic wave at Martin. The other lifted his eyebrows as they walked away.

"Well, that was rude," she admonished when they were out of earshot.

"So was the way he kept ogling your cleavage."

Ani gasped with outrage. "He was doing no such thing! I'll have you know, he offered to introduce me to some of the orchestra players once he learned I'm a pianist."

"I'll bet he did."

She paused as they reached the row of slot machines. Beeps and whistles sounded the air around them.

"What's that supposed to mean?"

"Did he even give you any kind of proof?"

"Proof?"

Adam dropped several chips into the slot and pulled the arm lever. Nothing. "Let me get this straight—he found out you're a professional pianist and told you he just happens to work at the casino's opera house?"

She lifted her chin. "That's right. And you were incredibly rude to him." She reached inside her clutch purse. "And as far as proof, here's his card."

Adam squinted in the dim lighting to study it. Looked real, all right. "Huh."

She didn't respond, just grabbed the bucket out of his hands and stormed over to another machine.

Adam rubbed his forehead. Damn it. He'd just acted like an uncultured brute, dragging his woman away from a male who'd shown her interest.

His woman?

He refused to analyze that thought. Sighing, he walked over to where Ani was playing three machines at once, inserting the maximum amount of chips in each one. She really was a bad gambler. One machine registered a handful of coins in return.

"You must really take me for a fool," she said without looking at him, her gaze focused on the flashing lights of the slot she was playing.

"That's not true. It just seemed too much of

a coincidence. And regardless of who he is, he was definitely ogling your cleavage." He hadn't imagined that part.

"Humph" was her only response.

Moments later, she turned the empty bucket upside down. "I appear to be out of chips."

"That took very little time. Would you like a drink?"

"Yes, I would like a drink and some air. I'll be outside."

Adam returned to the bar and ordered a bottle of champagne with two flutes. He could use a drink or two himself.

He found her by the lit fountain in front of the entrance. A rare, limited-issue Bentley pulled through the circular driveway before he could cross over to her.

When he did hand Ani a filled flute, she looked less than pleased with him. Her next question confirmed it. "That was quite embarrassing, Adam. Why did you behave that way in there? With Martin?"

He didn't really have an answer. Not a satisfactory one, anyway. He would have to tell her the truth—to admit that he'd been jealous.

"I mentioned his ogling, did I not?" He took a

long swig of the champagne. The highest quality this side of the Mediterranean, but he wasn't really tasting it. "I didn't like the way he was looking at you."

She turned to face him. "Well, that's something. Because it really bothered me the way some of those women in there were looking at you."

That was unexpected. "Huh."

She drained her glass in one impressive shot, then took the bottle from him to pour some more into her empty glass. "Maybe we need to figure this out, Adam."

"What's that?"

"Exactly what's happening between us."

Damned if I know, kitten.

Adam had whispered those words about three hours ago into her ear in answer to her loaded question. Only, it wasn't any kind of real answer.

Then he'd slowly lifted her chin and brushed his lips over hers ever so slightly.

Now, as she lay in bed with her window wide open, listening to the soft sounds of the night, she could almost feel herself back by the fountain in front of the Casino de Monte-Carlo. The taste of his lips still lingered on hers.

Like last night, she wasn't getting a wink of sleep. Insomnia had never particularly plagued her, but since arriving in Europe, she couldn't quite seem to get her mind to shut off when her head hit the pillow. It didn't help that Snowball was snoring in tempo, right by her head on top of the extra pillow.

But she mostly blamed Adam. Nearly all of her mind ramblings involved him in one way or another.

The moon cast a small glow of light about the room. A glance at the hanging wall clock told her it was 3:00 a.m. She may as well get some fresh air.

When she made it outside to the brick patio, she was surprised to find herself not alone. Adam was swimming laps along the length of the infinity pool.

With half a mind to turn around, she realized he'd somehow sensed her there and was looking right at her. She moved to the pool deck.

Adam swam to the edge where she stood above him. "Did I wake you?"

"No. I couldn't sleep." She crouched down to get closer to his eye level. "You either, huh?"

He brushed the hair off his face. The moonlight added a navy sheen to his wet, black hair. The way he had his arms braced on the edge of the pool accentuated the toned muscles of his chest and arms. Ani's fingers itched to touch him.

"Not uncommon. A lot of things keep me up at night."

The statement was so loaded and heavy, Ani longed to comfort him somehow. She had to remember he'd been an army officer deployed overseas. His nightmares were likely real memories of awful scenes he'd witnessed. She thought of all the times she would catch Brant staring off into space as one shudder after another rocked her brother's solid frame. He never wanted to talk about the terrors that caused it.

What horrors the two of them must have seen.

"A middle-of-the-night swim can do wonders to soothe the weary soul," Adam added.

"Is that so?"

"Most definitely. You should try it. Go grab your suit." His gaze fell to her bare thighs, then traveled up. "Or you could just jump in as you are."

Ani resisted the urge to cross her arms over her breasts. She should have grabbed some type of cover. The satin sleep set she wore was thin and flimsy and left very little to the imagination, especially around the vicinity of her chest. But it wasn't as if she'd expected to run into Adam at three in the morning.

What she ought to do was bid him good-night and rush back to her room.

But it did feel nice out here. The night was balmy with just a hint of a breeze. And they only had one more full night here. She didn't want to leave just yet.

"I think I'll just soak my feet."

She stood and walked over to the concrete steps that led into the pool, going as far as the third step, then sitting on the side edge. Adam swam over to join her at that end.

"Do you want to talk about it?" she asked when he reached her. He was perilously close to her left leg. She could feel the warmth of his skin against her knee. "What keeps you up at night, I mean?"

He rubbed his eyes. "Trust me, you don't want to hear about it."

"That doesn't mean I can't. My shoulders can bear more weight than you might think, Adam. I can lend you one. Or both."

Okay, it was a lame thing to say. But she meant it. Whatever else was happening between them, she liked to think they'd gotten close enough as individuals to trust and confide in each other.

He rested his arms on the wall, and his elbow touched her thigh. "I don't think I'd know where to start, kitten."

She'd apologized to him earlier about prying, but she found herself on the brink of doing it again nevertheless. She chewed on her bottom lip until it ached, concerned about his potential reaction to the question she was about to ask. "You could start by answering a question for me."

"What's that?"

"Why'd you really bring me here?"

"You've been wondering about that, have you?"

"Yes," she admitted. "You had to know I

would. You said something back in Paris about not wanting to repeat a past mistake."

"I shouldn't have said that," he said through gritted teeth. "It's history that should stay well in the past."

"History has a way of creeping into the present. Like when it keeps you awake at night."

His shoulders dropped. "You're right."

She sucked in a deep breath for the courage. She had to continue now that she'd started this. "Tell me, Adam."

Adam squeezed his eyes shut, the pain etched into his features visible even in the soft light.

Ani would have done anything to ease the pain emanating from him. If only she knew what that might be. "What mistake were you referring to?" she asked quietly.

Even under the water, she could sense Adam's entire body clench with tension. The anguish practically vibrated off him.

"The one where the woman I wanted to marry almost lost her life because of me."

The air around them seemed to still completely. Whatever had happened with this woman, Adam was carrying a palatable amount of guilt about it.

Despite the myriad of questions hammering in her brain, Ani remained unmoving and silent, giving Adam the full choice of how and if he wanted to continue.

"We were in a small province to secure the perimeter after enemy troops had fallen back. Troops who were defeated, but they still left their hidden traps and weapons behind them."

Ani swallowed past a painful lump that had formed at the base of her throat.

"A journalist for an Atlanta-based news agency and her cameraman were granted authorization to embed with our infantry," he continued, staring off into the distance. "She came often over the span of a few months to cover the story. We grew close."

Ani didn't need him to paint a picture. She could see where this was going.

"I was the officer in charge the last day we went out. She joined us to file a report and have her cameraman film."

"What happened?"

"She wasn't supposed to be there. I'd told her no at first. Something didn't feel right. There'd been rumors of renewed hostile activity. But I let her convince me ultimately because of our personal relationship. She wanted her story. I relented because she talked me into it. Because she told me I was holding her back. Just like my—"

He didn't finish his sentence but Ani could guess what he'd been about to say. His mother had walked out on him, no doubt accusing him of holding her back from the life she wanted to lead. One without a child weighing her down.

Adam sucked in a deep breath and rubbed his forehead before continuing. "We were traveling in an armored vehicle. I let her open the hatch just enough for her cameraman to take a quick photo. That's precisely the moment we hit the improvised explosive."

"Oh, Adam."

"She was critically injured, as was the cameraman. The surgical team at the military hospital on-site was able to save her but she suffered permanent injuries and scars. Luckily she's made a full recovery, though it was a long road."

"What else?" Ani prompted.

"I went to see her as soon as I got permission, ready to drop on one knee. Had the ring and everything."

Ani fought back the stinging in her eyes. The thought of Adam being ready to commit to someone else caused a sharp pain around the area of her heart. Still, she had to ask her next question. She had to know. "What happened?"

"Tried walking into her room but was stopped by a wall of family and friends. She refused to see me."

Ani couldn't hide her gasp of surprise.

Adam went on, "I can't blame her for wanting nothing to do with me." He pushed himself off the wall and back into the water. "But all that mattered was that she was going to be okay. I walked away and never contacted her again. Heard a few years later that she married her high school sweetheart and became an elementary school teacher."

He made his way back to the bottom step and began to climb out of the pool. Ani's hands were trembling as she reached for a towel tossed over the railing. She stood and handed it to him. They stood face-to-face, the height difference mitigated as she remained on the top while he was two steps below.

"Adam, you can't blame yourself for what

happened," she insisted, knowing full well he would pay her words no heed.

He took the towel from her, his fingers brushing hers. "Thank you for that, kitten. But I know what I did and all the ways I fell short in my responsibility."

Ani wanted to stomp her foot in protest. He'd been blaming herself all these years for something he couldn't have controlled. "I'm glad your reporter is okay," she said instead. "I'm glad she recovered fully. I'm sure she was hurt and scared and had her reasons for not wanting to see you. Reasons I guess I wouldn't understand."

"What's that mean?" he asked on a low whisper.

Ani swallowed through a throat that had suddenly gone dry. "It means I can't understand how any woman could just let you go."

Adam lifted an eyebrow. Rather than pull his hand back from where he'd reached for the towel, he grasped her wrist instead and pulled her closer. "You have to be careful about saying such things to me, kitten. Words like that might have consequences."

As if daring him, she stepped even closer,

feeling the length of him against the thin satin of her top. Her body immediately responded through the fabric.

Adam noticed.

"Maybe I'm ready for consequences," she whispered breathlessly, hardly recognizing her own voice.

Still he made no move. She would have to take matters into her own hands. She wanted him and she was tired of waiting.

Thrusting her hand into his hair, she pulled his face to hers and claimed his mouth. She'd never been so bold with a man, so achy to have him kiss her and hold her.

Adam might not have made the first move, but his reaction was immediate and fierce. Lifting her by the backs of her legs, he hoisted her up and took her to the closest lounge cot.

Ani could hardly breathe. He was gentle, attentive. Completely in tune with her at every moment. Her skin burned everywhere he touched her, everywhere he kissed her. She'd been dreaming of this, imagining the way he would feel when he loved her. But nothing could have prepared her for the reality of it.

By the time he carried her upstairs and into

his bed, she was nearly delirious with pleasure and need.

The consequences Adam had warned her of continued well past dawn.

It felt like déjà vu. Ani had awoken to an empty bed.

As disappointed as she was not to have Adam's warm body to snuggle into, she knew he was an early morning runner. She'd immediately gotten Snowball from her room and was with him on the grassy patch of yard with him now as she watched Adam jog up the stone pathway.

Just like yesterday. Only her world was so much different now. Adam Steele had made love to her. Her body reacted in response to the thought.

Judging by the sweaty look of him, he hadn't taken it easy on his run. Where did the man get such energy? Especially considering he'd been swimming in the middle of the night, and then not to mention all their shared activities afterward. A blush crept down her cheeks clear to her neck.

He stopped several feet in front of her. Snowball let out a small whimper. He'd noticed it, too—no pat on the head for her dog this morning. In fact, Adam's entire being stood rigid and tense. He wasn't quite meeting her eyes.

This did not bode well.

"Will you be ready to leave in a couple of hours?" he asked, without so much as a good morning.

Ani's heart sank. She refused to believe the worst just yet, but she was certainly beginning to suspect it. She nodded. "Not much to pack, after all."

He crossed his arms in front of his chest. Everything about him was closed off, resistant. "Good. That's good. We'll get you back to Paris to rejoin your team and the security detail. Then we can head to Brussels with plenty of time leftover."

Snowball went to rub against his ankle, begging to be acknowledged.

Same here, buddy.

Adam glanced down as if finally noticing the dog for the first time. Finally, he bent to give him a playful rub along his fur. When he straightened, he finally did meet her gaze. But his eyes held no warmth, and zero of the passion he'd shown himself to be capable of last night.

She knew she was being too silent, but for the life of her she couldn't come up with a thing to say. Also, she feared the risk of sobbing out loud and uncontrollably if she so much as opened her mouth. So she stood there, dumbstruck.

She could almost see the proverbial curtain he'd pulled between them. Why couldn't the man understand what was so clear to her? Up until now, she hadn't even realized she'd been missing having love or passion in her life. Now that she'd experienced it, she didn't think she could bear to lose it. To lose Adam.

"He must have missed you last night." Adam pointed to the dog.

Finally, an acknowledgment of what had happened between them. Ani cleared her throat before attempting to speak. "I don't think he noticed I was gone. Found him still curled up and snoring soundly when I got back."

He shoved his hair off his forehead, glanced out toward the ocean. "Good. That's good."

Ani tried to cling to some semblance of hope. It was a good sign, after all, that he'd been worried about her dog. But his next words threw cold water on that. "Look, Ani. I know we need to talk about all this. But I figure we should just focus on getting ready for the return to Paris right now. We can talk as we fly back."

What was there to talk about? Ani knew better than to ask. There was no reason to discuss what they'd shared last night unless he regretted it.

"I'm gonna go shower. I'll meet you up front when you're ready. The jet's waiting at the airport."

Ani felt the burn of tears behind her eyes and watched his back as he went into the house.

Looked like she'd be adding another discarded gown to Adam's guest closet.

Adam turned the hot water on as high as it would go and stepped into the shower stall. He'd already punished himself with a particularly harsh run and now he would punish himself with a near-scalding shower.

He'd been a selfish bastard for so much as touching Ani.

She was brightness and light and positivity. Whereas all he'd ever known was darkness throughout his life. He had no business risking that any of that darkness would touch her in any way. He should have stayed the hell away from her.

She'd paid him a compliment and he'd basically turned into a pile of desire and longing. And he'd lost control altogether when she'd pulled his mouth to hers and kissed him as hard as she had. Even now, his body reacted to the memory of that kiss in ways that had him groaning in need and frustration. Maybe a cold shower would have been a better option. He had to stop thinking about Ani Terrance in any way that wasn't strictly professional.

He'd been entrusted to protect her and look what he'd done instead.

Oh, and there was that whole thing about never being able to look Brant in the eye ever again. He would have to come clean with his friend. Couldn't risk the other man finding out some other way. And he'd just have to brace himself for Brant's inevitable right hook that Adam wouldn't return nor so much as duck. He deserved no less.

He cursed out loud and punched the tile wall

hard enough that his knuckles throbbed. What a complete mess.

Even if it took the self-restraint of a million monks, he absolutely could not touch her again. In fact, after her performance in Brussels, he would get her safely back to the States and then he would bid her goodbye. Raj and April could take over any remaining security needs for Ms. Terrance, including tracking down the sender of the blasted emails that had started this whole strange turn of events.

But first, he had to get her back to Paris. On a private plane, just the two of them. Mostly alone in the cabin.

One thing was certain: their flight back to France was bound to be a memorable one.

Ani wanted to forget everything about this return flight. With Adam working diligently on his laptop, she'd been feigning sleep in order to avoid talking to him. But that was getting old. And she knew she wasn't going to fool him much longer.

There was no point in having the discussion Adam was looking to have. Other than to make him feel better. It would make her feel considerably worse, if that was possible. She didn't need to hear about how it had all been a mistake. How one thing had led to another and how he should have exercised more constraint.

She stole a glance at him now through her partially shuttered eyelids. Even now, the sight of him tugged at her heart. What she wouldn't give to approach him, settle herself in his lap and ask for the comfort and solace she knew he could provide. If he'd only let himself.

But he wasn't ready to do that. He'd pulled himself away and shut himself off so completely, she knew it in no uncertain terms. Ani felt the sting of tears under her eyelids. This was exactly what she had meant to avoid. This feeling of loss and aching emptiness. She'd let herself fall for him when she had no business doing so. He wasn't ready to let anyone in; he was carrying too much of a burden. One he'd placed on his own shoulders and refused to put down.

She didn't think she had what it would take to reach him. She was too broken herself. Too confused about the reality she suddenly found herself in. Monaco had been a magical escape, a fantasy she couldn't hope to ever return to. Fantasies weren't real. Life didn't work that way.

Hers didn't, in any case. The gaping hole in her core left by the loss of her mother was proof of that. The magical time she'd spent with Adam had only been temporary, a brief respite. So she'd just continue to sit here and pretend to sleep until they reached the staunch, cold reality that awaited them back in Paris.

Except Snowball completely blew her cover. He suddenly jumped from his curled position on her lap and gave her a kiss that was overly wet even by his standards. Ani startled. Her eyes flew open.

Adam noticed immediately. "You're awake."

"Snowball seems to have wanted it that way."

"So I saw. He even jumps like a bunny," he teased, but Ani couldn't quite bring herself to smile and Adam's tight one seemed less than genuine.

"Can I get you anything?" he asked.

"Some water would be nice."

He got one from the bar and tossed it to her. "Listen, Ani—"

But she cut him off, feigning a nonchalance she didn't feel even as her heart continued to shatter in her chest. "I know what you're going to say."

"You do, huh?"

"I can guess. But I'd like to say something first."

His lips tightened before he responded, "Go ahead."

Now that she'd started, Ani wasn't sure how exactly she wanted to continue. "You're an incredible, accomplished man, Adam. I wish you could see that the way I do." She bit her lip before continuing, "I believe with all my heart that the woman you once wanted to marry has forgiven you. She's clearly moved on. Maybe it's time you allowed yourself to do the same."

He blew out a long breath. When he spoke, he didn't acknowledge anything she'd just said. It didn't surprise her. "Ani, I never meant for things to become this complicated."

Ani tried to breathe through the hollow churn of disappointment in her gut. Adam wasn't even going to broach the possibility of forgiving himself. And she wasn't sure how else to push. Or even if she should.

"I know. I just need to get past this next performance. Then we can address all the ways we're so wrong for each other and why we should go our separate ways."

He studied her features. "How'd your call with Moira go?"

Touché. Adam's question was his not-so-subtle way of pointing out that she was doing her own avoidance of sorts. They both knew Ani had never made that call.

She looked out the window, hoping he'd get the hint. This conversation was over before it had started. For now, at least.

CHAPTER ELEVEN

PERFORMING THIS TIME felt different.

Ani took the stage at the Forest National arena near Brussels and bowed before sitting in front of the piano and addressing the audience. She definitely felt less nervous than she had in Paris. After all, she'd done this once before and had triumphed.

Adam stood to the side of the stage, speaking into his earpiece and surveying the audience. He looked devastatingly handsome in the navy, Italian-cut suit. He turned to her and gave her a small wink before she walked out to play, making her heart lurch in her chest. He'd stayed away from her since they'd returned from Monte Carlo. April and Raj had taken over most of her detail.

Much to her dismay, she'd cried about that both nights until she fell asleep. She missed him. Somehow, when she hadn't been paying attention, she'd gone and fallen genuinely in love with her childhood crush. Or maybe she'd been in love with him all along. Whereas Adam had been avoiding an attraction to her all those years ago, she'd already started giving him her heart. There was no doubt now that it belonged to him fully and probably always would.

And wasn't this a fine time to be thinking about her foolishness when it came to Adam Steele?

Ani focused on the keys and began her first number.

The next two hours seemed to go by in a flash and before she knew it, she was taking her encore bow. April whisked her off the stage as soon as the curtain closed. Adam was nowhere to be seen. Just as well. He'd made his decision and Ani wasn't one to grovel.

Somehow, someway, she would get over the hurt of losing him. No doubt it would take time. Years, perhaps.

Once she reached the backstage dressing room, she shut the door behind her and leaned against it. Moira's knock came within seconds, but Ani chose to ignore it. She just needed some time to breathe.

It was over. She'd fulfilled her contractual

commitments and her shows had been a notable success judging from the standing ovation out there.

But one thing was certain: she wasn't ready to make this a full-time career. She simply didn't want this kind of lifestyle. She liked having a home base and being able to volunteer her time where she was needed. She was going to have to turn down offers to continue touring. Moira would be disappointed, but this was Ani's life and she had to do what was right for her.

She hoped her mother would agree if she were here.

Her life plan was still an uncharted mystery, but at least she knew what she didn't want. As for what she did want… She thought of Adam once more and her heart fluttered in her chest despite herself. It had hurt just to look at him standing offstage. What she wanted most appeared to be out of her reach.

Adam forced himself to stay away from Ani's door. Her last performance was over. Which meant that in less than two days, his contractual obligation to protect her would also be complete.

Along the same lines, his IT guy had informed him that they were narrowing in on the server location where the mysterious emails had been sent. Pretty soon, they'd have a solid identity and neutralize any kind of threat. She'd have no need for him once that happened.

Judging by her performance just now and after the one in Paris, Ani was certain to have the whole world at her feet with her talent as a musician.

There'd be no holding her back.

The knock came again about an hour later. Ani gave in with resignation and went to answer the door. She had to let Moira in sometime.

But it was April on the other side of the door. "Hey."

"Hey. Come on in."

April strode into the room and pulled a bouquet of flowers from behind her back. "This is from all of us on your security detail to congratulate you. Way to knock 'em dead. In Paris, too."

Ani took the arrangement and inhaled the wonderful aroma, beyond touched at the gesture.

"And the boss says to tell ya 'good job.'"

Ani stilled in the process of putting the flowers in a tall glass of water. "Oh, he did, did he? Did he happen to mention why he won't come down here and tell me himself?"

April bounced on her heels. "Uh... I dunno. I don't really ask him questions of that nature."

Ani released her outrage on a sigh. "Sorry, April. He and I haven't exactly been communicating. Guess he wants to keep it that way."

April scratched the back of her head. "It's probably not my place to say, and I have no idea what's going on between you two. But for what it's worth, he seems pretty miserable."

Well, that was some small source of satisfaction.

"Also, for what it's worth, the flowers were his idea."

Rather than placating her, April's statement had the opposite effect. Of all the nerve! He couldn't come down here to congratulate her and he'd sent someone else to deliver the flowers he'd thought to get. As if they hadn't been as intimate as two people could be just two short nights ago.

Ani felt her blood pressure rise by several units. "I see. Is he still in the building?"

April nodded. "We don't leave until you're ready to."

Ani pointed to April's earpiece. "Could you radio him and ask him to come to my dressing room, please? Tell him it's urgent."

When Adam arrived less than five minutes later, Ani had only grown more steamed.

"You summoned?" he asked.

"Only because it didn't occur to you to come on your own."

April was smart enough to make a hasty exit as soon as they began their snarky exchange.

"Was there something you needed?" Adam asked as April shut the door behind her.

"Yes. I need to know why you've been avoiding me."

She also needed to stop noticing how devilishly handsome he looked. He'd taken off the suit jacket and rolled up his sleeves. The top three buttons of his shirt were undone and revealed enough of his chest that she remembered running her hands over and kissing that exact spot. She shook her head.

"I haven't been avoiding you," he protested.

"You didn't even bring me the flowers you bought yourself."

He crossed his arms in front of his chest and widened his feet, apparently ready to do battle. Well, so was she.

"You said on the plane ride that you'd rather not talk," he said. "I guess I was supposed to know you changed your mind about that."

"You were supposed to ask, Adam."

"Fine. I'll ask. Do you want to talk?"

If Ani was holding anything, she would have been tempted to throw it at him. "Yes, let's talk," she said, angry. "Go ahead and tell me how this thing between us will never work. That we're too different and you have no room in your life right now for any kind of relationship."

He lifted an eyebrow at her.

"I'm right, aren't I?" she pressed. "All that is pretty much what you intended to say."

"You are," he admitted. "That doesn't make any of it less true."

Why was she pursuing this? Why was she even going down this path, knowing full well it was only going to lead to further heartbreak? It was all so pointless. She didn't have what it would take to reach him.

Still, the words continued to flow out of her

mouth. Deep down, some deeply seated need within her wanted to try. "You were abandoned by your mother, then made a mistake with a woman you were in love with. A mistake that you can't get over. And it's making you turn your back on what could be a really good thing." She clenched her fists by her sides. "Just because you're scared to move forward and try for happiness."

"Do we really want to talk about who's scared, Ani?"

The thick, heavy tone of his voice sent alarm bells ringing in her head.

"I could go ahead and tell you what I think," he offered.

She flung out her arms, palms up. "By all means."

"You spent the whole time in Monaco avoiding talking to Moira. You're on the precipice of this opportunity that most artists can only dream of. And you can't figure out how to proceed. Why are you so afraid of making a decision and then just sticking to it?"

How could he ask her such a thing? "Not everyone is cut out to live a public life. Can you blame me for grappling with that?"

"Of course not. So accept that about yourself and say no."

He couldn't understand. He had no idea how it felt to lose the woman who had started her on the journey to becoming a musician. In addition to being her parent, her mother had been a source of support and nurturing and teaching. A true mentor. "It's not as easy as you seem to think. I had to consider what my mother would say. She was my first instructor. If it wasn't for her, I wouldn't even be a musician."

"And now her absence is a convenient excuse."

The blood drained from her face. "What?"

"An excuse to stay precisely where you are without ever having to decide."

Ani wanted to believe she hadn't heard him correctly. But the ringing in her ears hadn't muddled his words. He'd been loud and clear.

She could throw it in his face how wrong he was, that she *had* decided in fact. And that she was figuring out how to tell Moira about her rejection of the offers.

There was no point. He saw her as a spoiled and coddled child unable to steer her own life.

"Get out, Adam."

He cursed and reached for her, the regret clear in his dark eyes. "Ani, I didn't mean—"

She held a hand up before he could continue, and stepped out of his reach. "Please. Just leave."

As if he needed any more confirmation that he could be an insufferable bastard. He'd gone over and over the whole scene with Ani as he'd tossed and turned all night. He would take it back if he could.

Adam waited until the morning to try to set things right with her. He'd been completely out of line and lashed out. All because she'd spoken the truth. And he hadn't been able to take it. For a hardened soldier who'd seen more than his share of travesty, he hadn't been able to cope when the woman he'd cared for his entire life had held a mirror up to him and asked him to face his past.

He would tell her all that as soon as he saw her.

Hopefully, the hours of sleep had taken some of the edge off her anger. Not that he deserved any kind of leeway. He'd been way out of line. And he needed to tell her that.

No one answered when he knocked on her hotel suite door.

He walked down two doors to Moira's room. Maybe they were having breakfast together.

But Moira was alone when she answered. Unless you counted Snowball, who ran over to him barking, then rubbed against his ankle. Adam crouched down to give him a quick pet but he rolled over onto his back and kicked his leg up in the air.

He was particularly needy this morning. Adam proceeded with an obligatory belly rub. Moira was glaring at him when he straightened.

"Where is she?" he asked. "I'm in charge of her security. I need to know."

He could have sworn Moira sneered before answering. "She's not here. She left."

A heavy weight settled over his shoulders. "Left? Where to?"

"Took a commercial flight back to the States last night. Asked me to watch Snowball and bring him back with us so she wouldn't have to crate him on the plane."

Adam felt his gut tighten. He'd driven her away. Another strike on his already tarnished existence. "She's not supposed to travel any-where without Steele Security officers."

Moira leaned over and picked up the dog, who proceeded to lick her without pause. "She didn't. April took her."

Was he the only one Ani had kept in the dark about her plans to leave? Adam swore out loud and called up April's number on his phone. Moira stood watching from the doorway with both derision and unhidden interest.

April answered on the first ring. "Hey, boss. What took you so long to call?"

"Care to tell me what's going on?"

He could practically see her characteristic shrug through the phone. "Simple. She wanted to leave. Told me you'd have a 'tantrum'—her word—if she traveled to the airport without se-curity, so I took her. And with all due respect, you can fire me if you want. But us girls gotta stick together."

Adam rubbed his forehead where the begin-ning of a pounding headache was starting to set in. "I wished you'd told me, April."

"She asked me not to. And I like Ani."

Yeah, so did he. And he'd blown it with her. He knew there couldn't be a future between them, but it was tearing him to shreds inside that she would hate him now for the foreseeable future. And she had every right to.

"So are you gonna?" April asked through the tinny speaker.

"Am I going to what?"

"Fire me?"

"No, April. I'm not going to fire you."

Her sigh of relief was audible through the call. She thanked him profusely before hanging up.

Not that he was due any gratitude.

"She wanted to get home to work on some audition pieces. That's what she said, anyway." The hint of blame was clear in Moira's voice. She would be right. This was his fault. Adam could guess why Ani wanted to get home a day early: to avoid him.

Moira put the dog down midlick. He scrambled away and jumped up on the couch, whimpering as if he was missing something.

Yeah, I miss her too, pal.

The first part of Moira's comment registered in his brain. "What audition pieces?"

"She's looking to audition for some orchestra positions throughout the States. Maybe even in

Europe. That way she can still be a performing musician but she doesn't have to tour or deal with publicity headaches. She said she got the suggestion from someone she met in Monte Carlo at some casino you took her to."

The theater manager she met at the bar that night. And he'd accused her of being naive for believing the man.

Adam wanted to punch a wall. He'd accused her of being afraid to move forward. The reality was that not only had she moved forward, she'd figured out a path without compromising anything of herself or squandering her great talent. She hadn't even bothered to set him straight because he simply wasn't worth it. Not after the unforgivable words he'd spewed at her.

"Anyway," Moira went on, "I'm glad you're not going to fire April."

He could only nod. Of course he wasn't going to fire her. The only person who deserved any kind of punishment in all this was himself. And losing Ani so completely, without any hope of winning her back, would feel like a penance for the rest of his days.

CHAPTER TWELVE

ADAM WASN'T LOOKING forward to this meeting, even less than the one he'd agreed to over two weeks ago when he'd gone to see Brant and Mr. Terrance. So much could change in a matter of days. And so much could stay exactly the same. The same receptionist was seated at the outer desk when Adam made it to the top floor. Like the last time, she motioned him in.

Brant stood up from his desk and came over to give him a big bear hug when Adam entered his office. Probably the last hug he'd receive from his oldest and closest friend. Yet another painful personal loss he would have to endure. And he had no one but himself to blame.

Adam had to accept that things would be different between them after this conversation.

Brant motioned for him to sit in the chair opposite his own.

"So Ani's performances were both a huge

success, it sounds like," Brant began, dropping down into his own seat.

"They were. Everything went smoothly."

"I got your message about tracing those suspicious emails," his friend said. "Nice work figuring it out."

Adam nodded. "Turns out they were sent to her from one of her music students. He meant no harm. Just figured she might find it flattering to have a secret admirer. The poor kid didn't exactly think it through."

"I guess not."

"The counselors at the center made sure to speak with him about the inappropriateness of his actions. He feels terrible."

Adam had sent the same message to Ani to notify her of the discovery his investigation had unearthed. She hadn't responded.

"The kid's got some impressive technical skills," Adam continued. "Hacked into the youth center's Wi-Fi to access their contact list. It's how he obtained Ani's updated email address."

"Well, leave it to my sister," Brant said. "Not only has she forgiven him, she convinced the center not to pursue any kind of charges. And she personally took the kid to sign him up for a local coding class."

Adam wasn't surprised in the least. That sounded like the woman he'd fallen for. The woman he'd foolishly managed to lose.

"I'm just glad it's all over," Brant added. "But better safe than sorry. Especially when it comes to loved ones."

"Some things are too precious to risk," he agreed, well aware of the irony of his words.

"So tell me about Ani's concerts," Brant prompted. "I was really hoping to fly to Europe to catch one, but this merger has hit one snag after another. The timing just wasn't right. Dad and I both felt terrible about missing the chance to see her."

"She blew both audiences away."

Brant's grin grew wider. "That's my sis."

"She's something else."

"She really is. And I hear you took her to spend some time at your villa in Monaco. That was above and beyond, man."

Adam shifted in his seat. "We should probably talk about that."

"Yeah?"

"The truth is, Ani and I became close during the Monaco visit."

"Close?"

"Real close. I'm not sure how else to put it."

Brant crossed his ankle over his knee. "I see."

Adam cleared his throat. "So, just give me some warning. So that I can brace for the blow. That's all I ask."

Brant squinted his eyes. "What in the devil's name are you talking about?"

"When you land the first punch. I just want to be prepared."

"You think I'm going to punch you? Why would I want to do that?"

"Because of what I just told you. That Ani and I—"

Brant jumped up before Adam could continue. "Whoa, whoa. I don't need to hear the details, brother."

Adam ducked his head. This conversation was even more awkward than he'd feared.

"Just fair warning, though," Brant said.

"What's that?"

"I reserve the right to change my mind about that punch if it turns out you've taken advantage of her in any way. Buddy or not."

Brant's statement was no less than what he'd expected. Still, Adam felt a brush of ire rustle up his spine. "She's been taken advantage of, all right. Probably her whole life."

Brant stiffened where he stood. "What's that supposed to mean?"

"You really don't see it, do you? Nor does your dad, I bet. Neither of you ever have."

"See what?" Brant demanded.

"Everything Ani's been to you both since the loss of your mom. How strong she's been. How she's held you up. Both of you. You both would have fallen apart without her. You've been blind to all her sacrifices."

Brant's eyes narrowed to ominous slits. "I don't need you to extol the virtues of my sister. I know all she's done for us. Been to us."

"Do you really, Brant?"

A hint of color rose on the other man's cheeks. Someone who didn't know him as well as Adam might not have noticed. But there was no doubt Brant was angry.

Despite that, Adam continued, "Ani happens to be strong and resilient and caring. And she deserved more from her father and brother than to have to bear the burden of trying to dull your pain, on top of struggling with her own."

Several beats passed in the most uncomfortable silence he and Brant had ever experienced between them. And that was saying a lot.

Finally, Brant blew out a loud breath. "You're right. My sister is one of the most generous people I know. If it wasn't for her, my dad and I would have been even more of a mess after we lost Mom. She was the rock we both leaned on. She took care of everything. Even as young as she was and with how much she was grieving herself. It's past time we acknowledged that. Though we'll never be able to make it up to her."

Adam tilted his head in agreement. "She deserves to be happy."

"Sounds like you really care for her."

Adam had been coming to terms with that fact since she had left Brussels without him. He'd never felt such emptiness, or been so damn lonely, as he'd been after Moira had told him Ani was gone.

The only sound conclusion was that he not only cared for Ani, he'd fallen in love with her. He couldn't even say when. Perhaps he'd loved her since they were both kids and she insisted on trailing him and Brant until one of them told her to scram.

Adam looked Brant straight in the eye before he answered, "I always have. And I always will."

Brant nodded once. "Then why are you in here fighting on her behalf when you could be out there fighting *for* her?"

Adam leaned over, bracing his arms on his knees. "I think I may have blown it with her."

"You have a tendency to do that, don't you, bro?"

Just like that, the awkwardness between them dissipated like mist in the air. His friend had never been afraid to tell it like it was. It was a quality Adam both admired and dreaded being on the receiving end of.

"And if I know you," Brant continued, "you're probably wracking your brain for what to do about it when the answer is so very obvious."

At Adam's blank stare, Brant threw his arms up in the air. It was a gesture reminiscent of his sister's. "Just go see her, man. Sounds like you both could use some clearing of the air."

Brant was right. Regardless of where it would

lead, apologizing to her face-to-face was the least Adam could do. But ultimately, it was her call to make. "I'll try. If she agrees to give me the time of day, that is."

"She'll give you a chance. If you deserve it," Brant declared.

That was the question, wasn't it? Whether Adam deserved her at all.

He had to find out. Even if it meant he might never recover once he learned the answer. He was about to shut the door behind him when Brant's final comment gave him pause.

"You deserve to be happy, too, Adam."

Adam paused in the act of ringing Ani's doorbell. The faint piano music he could hear coming through her door had him straining to hear. The piece was unfamiliar to his ears. She hadn't performed this one in Paris nor Brussels. He would have remembered. It was stunning.

The tempo was upbeat, yet somehow a sadness resounded through the musical notes. Even without lyrics, the song spoke of desire. Of loss and pain.

Or maybe he was a fanciful clod who'd gone

and lost his heart and now he was hearing po-
etry everywhere.

He wasn't sure how long he stood there. He
just knew he couldn't interrupt her, had to hear
the melody to its conclusion.

When Ani stopped playing, he inhaled a for-
tifying breath and rang her bell.

He heard shuffling on the other side. Yet
the door didn't open. She must have seen him
through the peephole but wasn't responding.

Served him right. He shouldn't have come un-
announced. He felt his hope deflate like a punc-
tured balloon. She was going to ignore him.

He opened his mouth to try to reason with her
through the door, but couldn't seem to find the
right words. All the lines he'd rehearsed back
at home seemed inadequate now. He braced
both hands on opposite sides of the doorway
and resigned himself to the facts—this time,
the damage he'd caused was irreparable. And
he would have to live with that.

He turned around to leave.

Ani stood frozen in front of her door, torn as
to what to do. She longed to see Adam, to talk
to him. She longed to be in his arms again.

But her emotions were still too raw, and she had a piece to finish if she was going to be ready for this first audition.

Still, she'd missed him so much. Hadn't been able to stop thinking about him since arriving back home. He'd texted and left voice mails but she hadn't had the fortitude to try to answer. And now he was here in person.

She watched through the peephole as he stood there, simply waiting. Even through the distorted view, her breath caught at how handsome he was.

She flung the door open before she could change her mind, catching him just as he was turning to leave.

"You didn't try very hard," she said with as steady a voice as she could muster. "Only rang the doorbell once."

He flashed that charming smile of his she'd missed so much. He was dressed casually in khakis and a soft white V-neck. Dark stubble covered his strong jawline. She itched to reach out and run her fingertips over it.

"I was going to come back with a bouquet," he said. "Flowers convinced you to see me last time."

She looked upward as if contemplating his statement. "Though that didn't end too well, did it?" she countered.

"Touché. Can I come in?"

She stepped aside and nearly reached out to touch him as he walked past her into the living room. The familiar scent of his aftershave brought forth memories of Paris and Monaco and all that they'd shared.

He walked over to her grand piano in the corner of the room. Trailed a finger along the keyboard. "That was an extraordinary piece you were playing when I arrived."

"I've been working on it all week. It's starting to come around."

"You wrote that?"

She nodded. "I did." Little did he know, he'd played a major part in the process. Ani had thought of him while creating the stanzas. She'd poured all the anguish, the longing, the loss she'd felt since leaving Brussels into the music.

"You're unbelievable, Ani. I don't know anything about music, but what I heard had me mesmerized outside your door."

She could only thank him. For several moments, they both simply stood in silence. Unspoken words hung heavily in the air between them. Ani wasn't going to budge. This was all on him.

"What's the name of the piece?" he finally asked.

Ani took a deep breath before responding. "Monaco Moonlight."

His eyes darkened when he heard her answer. He glanced from her to the music sheet. When he finally spoke, his voice was thick with raw emotion. "Ani, I've been such a blind idiot."

She crossed her arms in front of her chest. A desperate attempt to keep from rushing into his arms the way she so badly wanted to. She'd missed him so much. But he'd broken her heart that night in Brussels. In so many pieces. She was still in the process of trying to mend it. "You won't get any argument from me on that front."

"I was a fool to say the things I did. I was only protecting myself."

"Your duty was to protect me." Instead, he'd shattered her.

He visibly cringed. "I know. If you let me, I'll never forfeit that duty again. I promise."

"You pushed me away, Adam."

"I know, kitten. The truth is, I need protecting, too."

That was a bit of an unexpected curve. "You do?"

He reached for her, but Ani wasn't ready to accept the hand he offered. Not just yet. She stayed firm where she was, though every cell in her body cried out to go to him, to hell with the consequences.

"Ani, please save me from myself. Say you'll forgive me."

She felt the last bricks of her wall crumble, slowly but surely. She was fooling herself to think she could deny what she felt for him, that she'd ever be able to get over him in this lifetime. How did she have any recourse but to forgive him?

"I guess I don't have a choice," she said on a sigh with mock resignation.

"Yeah?"

She shook her head seriously. "It appears you've somehow managed to become my muse. I'll have to keep you around. In the interest of my professional growth."

He reached her in one quick stride, then lifted

her in his arms. Ani felt her whole body shudder with desire at being held by him again.

He trailed a line of soft kisses along her neck. "I can think of all sorts of ways to inspire you, kitten."

EPILOGUE

"IT'S MUCH WINDIER up here than I would have thought." Ani adjusted the tie holding her hair back, but it was no match for the wind. Several strands escaped again and whipped about her face.

"We are pretty high up." Adam stated the obvious.

"I can't believe we didn't come up here that first trip to Paris."

Ani glanced down at the breathtaking scene from the viewing deck of the Eiffel Tower. The stunning image would stay with her forever. The city lights framed by the majestic river could have been a painting hanging in a museum.

Adam took her in his arms from behind and rested his chin atop her head. He'd surprised her with a weeklong trip to France, followed by several days at his Monaco villa. Almost a replay of their first time here without any of the angst.

All to celebrate her latest successful audition. Ani hadn't quite decided if she would take the freelance opportunity with the Boston Pops Orchestra. The thought of leaving her beloved Dallas still had her torn.

The good news was, Adam had vowed to follow her wherever she wanted to go. And as long as he was by her side, she was home.

She snuggled tighter up against him. She wouldn't have thought it was possible to fall more in love with him over the past year, yet somehow she had.

Even after all this time, her heart still fluttered in her chest whenever he walked into a room. They stood there for several moments, enjoying the view and the night. She didn't think she'd ever felt this content.

Finally, Adam turned her around to face him. "So, I was thinking next time you go to Boston that I should come with you."

"I'd like that very much." She was planning to visit at least a couple more times before making her final decision.

"In fact, I think you should have your own personal bodyguard when you go."

She smiled at him with all the love filling her heart. "A girl can't be too careful."

"Exactly," he agreed and reached into his jacket pocket. Ani lost her breath when she saw the object he pulled out.

A small velvet box. He opened it to reveal a sparkling tear-shaped diamond ring on a tri-color gold band.

Ani clasped a shaky hand to her mouth. "Adam, it's lovely."

He took her hand in his, dropped a kiss to the inside of her wrist. "Anikita Terrance, you've been my top VIP for as long as I can remember. Would you please do me the honor of becoming my wife?"

Her whole body vibrated with pure happiness. She didn't think it was possible to feel this much joy. Throwing her arms around his neck, she finally managed to make her mouth work enough to give him an answer.

"Oui, mon amour! Yes!"

* * * * *

LET'S TALK
Romance

For exclusive extracts, competitions
and special offers, find us online:

- **f** facebook.com/millsandboon
- **◯** @millsandboonuk
- **𝕏** @millsandboon

Or get in touch on 0844 844 1351*

For all the latest titles coming soon,
visit millsandboon.co.uk/nextmonth

*Calls cost 7p per minute plus your phone company's price per
minute access charge

Kirklees
COUNCIL

Library and Information Centres
Red Doles Lane
Huddersfield, West Yorkshire
HD2 1YF

**This book should be returned on or before the latest date stamped below.
Fines are charged if the item is late.**

10|18

TEEN

**You may renew this loan for a further period by phone, personal visit or at
www.kirklees.gov.uk/libraries, provided that the book is not required by
another reader.**

NO MORE THAN THREE RENEWALS ARE PERMITTED

800677729

Praise for No Fixed Address

'Susin Nielsen is an amazing writer.
No Fixed Address is my book of the year'
Hilary McKay

'Susin Nielsen is the finest voice currently writing YA. Not many writers can put comedy and heartbreak in the same book, never mind the same page, but Susin does it effortlessly'
Phil Earle

'No Fixed Address tackles tough issues with endless humour and hope. A beautiful book'
Maximum Pop

'Susin Nielsen is warm, funny and doesn't write like anyone else'
Charlotte Eyre, The Bookseller

'No Fixed Address is another triumph from one of my absolute favourite writers'
Katie Clapham, Storytellers, Inc.

Praise for We Are All Made of Molecules

'A book to fortify readers against bullies and homophobes'
Sunday Times

'One to make you laugh, cry and read in one sitting'
The Bookseller

'Snappy and witty. A really fine YA novel'
Telegraph

'This is stellar, top-notch stuff'
Quill and Quire, starred review

'Unputdownable'
INIS

Praise for Optimists Die First

'Hilarious, heart-warming and beautifully unexpected – a real keeper'
Lisa Williamson

'Susin Nielsen has produced a richly comic story featuring a cast of mismatched, engaging characters'
Guardian

'Entertaining but also poignant'
Irish Times

'*Optimists Die First* is both funny and heartbreaking. Fans of
Rainbow Rowell's *Eleanor & Park* will love it'
Red Magazine

'Nielsen writes with sensitivity, empathy and humour'
Kirkus, starred review

'Grief and guilt permeate Nielsen's empathic and deeply moving
story, balanced by sharply funny narration and dialogue'
Publishers Weekly, starred review

PRAISE FOR *THE RELUCTANT JOURNAL OF HENRY K. LARSEN*

Winner of the Governor General's Literary Award, the UKLA
Award and the Canadian Library Association's Children's Book of
the Year

'A realistic, poignant portrait of one teen who overcomes nearly
unbearable feelings of grief and guilt'
Kirkus

'A fantastic narrator, authentic and endearing . . . a memorable
read for all the right reasons'
BookTrust

PRAISE FOR *Word Nerd*

'Ingenious and warm-hearted, Nielsen's writing boasts
believable, unpredictable characterisation'
Guardian

'Ambrose Bukowski is the titular nerd and it's in his delightful,
disarming voice that *Word Nerd* unfolds . . . a funny, wry tale'
Globe and Mail

PRAISE FOR *My Messed-Up Life*

'Sassy and candid'
Publishers Weekly, starred review

'Laugh-out-loud humour deftly mixes with insight . . .
This comic novel scores'
Kirkus